DEAD RECKONING

DEAD RECKONING

By Julie Burtinshaw

RAINCOAST BOOKS

Vancouver

Raincoast Books acknowledges the ongoing support of The Canada Council; the British Columbia Ministry of Small Business, Tourism and Culture through the BC Arts Council; and the Government of Canada through the Book Publishing Industry Development Program (BPIDP).

First published in 2000 by

Raincoast Books
9050 Shaughnessy Street
Vancouver, B.C.
V6P 6E5
(604) 323-7100
www.raincoast.com

Edited by Joy Gugeler
Typeset by Bamboo & Silk Design Inc.
Cover design by Leslie Smith
Cover art by John Macdonald

1 2 3 4 5 6 7 8 9 10

CANADIAN CATALOGUING IN PUBLICATION DATA
     Burtinshaw, Julie, 1958-
     Dead reckoning
     ISBN 1-55192-342-4
     1. Valencia (Steamer)—Juvenile fiction. I. Title.
     PS8553.U69623D42 2000   jC813'.6   C00-910706-1
     PZ7.B94568De 2000

Printed and bound in Canada

To my parents,
Maggie Garrett-Burtinshaw and
Charles Burtinshaw,
who gave me the courage to dream.

And to Joy Gugeler
for her thoughtfulness, patience and
encouragement during this project.

CONTENTS

PROLOGUE

"A hermit," my mother had said. "A crazy old fool living by himself out there in the middle of nowhere."

He sat across from me now, clutching a worn leather scrapbook in his paper-thin hands. I had not seen him in 39 years, but I had come immediately when he had called — he was my great-grandfather, James Moffat.

My family had only visited him once, when I was a toddler, so I remembered very little. Somewhere, there is a picture of me perched on his much younger knee; in the picture he is smiling, but his eyes are vacant, anchored in a distant past.

When he spoke, his voice was as thin and fragile as a butterfly's wing. "There is a story I need to tell you," he said, holding up the old scrapbook. "It's in here," he said, patting its fraying cover, "and in here," tapping first his temples, then his heart.

We were in his ramshackle cottage on a desolate, windswept peninsula near Pachena Point, Vancouver

Island, overlooking a shore the locals called "The Graveyard of the Pacific."

His place was small — a home perched on the edge of the wilderness, barely clinging to the continent. A tangled first-growth forest crowded against its walls and the monstrous red cedars pressed it perilously close to the sheer cliffs that dropped menacingly to the Pacific below.

His house was sparsely furnished, but comfortable, filled with objects the ocean had tossed back — shells, stones, nets, buoys, old bottles. "Things she doesn't want," he mumbled.

Over the fireplace, protected by a cracked and dusty sheet of glass, hung a faded topographical map.

Great-grandfather stabbed the map with his shaking finger. "I came here when I was only a boy, and only for a short time, but the sea and this coast got into my blood and I knew I had no choice but to return."

But why? It was the most forlorn, isolated landscape I had ever seen.

While he was talking I paced in front of a gallery of old black-and-white photos of ships. I inspected each one, walking from picture to picture.

"Read the names of the ships aloud to me," Great-grandfather barked, suddenly impatient with my casual interest.

"The *Consort*. The *Anne Bernard*. The *William Tell*. The *Gem of the Ocean*. The *Malleville*. The *Webfoot*. The *Nellie May*. The *Highland Light*. The *Condor*. The *Mattewwan*. The *Kailua*. The *Renfrew*. The *Beryl*. The

Janet Crown. The *Thomas R. Foster*. The *Soquel*. The *King David*. So many ships," I said.

"All kinds," Great-grandfather croaked. "All sizes — motorboats, yachts, steamers, tugs, even a battleship from the Second World War."

One photo hung in a frame off to one side: the *Valencia*. The name seemed familiar to me, like the half-remembered words of a long-ago lullaby.

The tarnished plate beneath the picture read *1906*. The old photo was grainy, undefined. However, the *Valencia*, from the faded look of its dimensions, was a formidable ship.

"The *Valencia*," said Great-grandfather, "was a steamer I boarded in San Francisco. It brought me to this very spot."

I studied the photo closely. In it, the *Valencia* is anchored in San Francisco's port. It is 1906. People line the decks, more than 100 of them, waving and laughing at an invisible camera. They look expectant, unafraid.

"There I am," said Great-grandfather. "That's me."

I followed his finger. A boy, about 13 or 14 years old, sat in the ship's rigging. He gazed solemnly toward the camera lens, his small hands clinging to the thick rope.

"You?" I whispered and reached up to touch the boy's cheek through the glass. Strange heat radiated from the picture and I withdrew my hand quickly.

"Yes, she can do that to you," Great-grandfather breathed. "Even after all these years, something about the *Valencia* lives on."

I pulled my sweater more tightly around me. The air in the room was suddenly cold and I shivered, crouching closer to the fireplace.

"You're shaking," Great-grandfather said. "Come and sit down."

He settled his frail frame in the easy chair in the corner and opened the scrapbook to the first page.

"It's a story I've been afraid to tell, until now," he said. His tired eyes drifted about the room, then rested on mine. "The *Valencia*..." he began, "but I must go further back than that. I was born in San Francisco in 1892, in America, but not an American...."

ONE

All, all are gone,
the old familiar faces.

— CHARLES LAMB, "THE OLD FAMILIAR FACES"

James Moffat was drowning. He could feel himself being tugged beneath the churning force of gallons of dark water, but also toward a light, a future. He was in some half-world. When he awoke his breathing was shallow and raspy.

"It was just a dream," he reassured himself, lightly slapping arms and legs still rigid with fear. It took a few minutes for his eyes to become accustomed to the silvery light skidding through his windowpane and onto the white sheets. Once they adjusted to the darkness, he dropped his feet to the floor.

Without looking at a clock, he _knew_ it was five minutes past midnight. A bead of sweat trickled down his back. He inhaled, fighting to slow his thumping heart. He had the *same* dream, every night, at the *same* time. He could not remember the last time he had slept, undisturbed, through the night.

James wrapped his skinny arms around his trembling body, climbed out of bed and padded across the room to his window. It was slightly open and a warm, damp breeze fanned his clammy skin.

He pressed his forehead against the cool glass and gazed out at the tall, narrow houses that lined the street where he had been born. A lone wagon rolled slowly over the grey cobblestones, pulled by a boney old horse — otherwise the street was still. James shivered and stepped back, his toes sinking into the thick Persian carpet in front of the sill.

The vague outline of his skull left an imprint on the window. He traced it slowly with his finger — recognizing its eerie, skeletal likeness — at once him, but not him. He was cold and made a beeline back to bed.

The details of his nightmare clambered to the surface of his thoughts, but he pushed them away, turning his mind instead to the unexpected announcement his parents had made at dinner only a few evenings ago. It had taken him completely by surprise — if anything his parents did could still surprise him.

James briefly wondered, though not for the first time, what it would be like to be born into a *normal* family with fistfuls of brothers and sisters, a father who had a *regular* job and a mother who cared more about her children than about *bugs*.

James' parents dedicated their every waking moment to the pursuit of collecting and cataloguing insects. Entomology was a relatively new science and they were pioneers in the field, ready to travel to Canada on a specimen-collecting trip in search of rare breeds of *Papilionoidea,* commonly called the butterfly.

"We're moving, dear," his mother had announced, jumping up from her chair then sitting down again. "To Victoria, Canada. It's on an island, Vancouver Island. It's where your cousins live. Now, did I put the salt on the table?" she added, leaving her seat again.

"What?" James put his fork down and reached for the salt. "Here it is, Mother."

"Pardon, not *what,*" his mother corrected. "I said we are moving. You should try to listen when I speak to you." She took the saltshaker and wandered off in the general direction of the parlour. "Where did I put my book?" she murmured to herself.

"Dad?" James looked at his father pleadingly.

John Moffat took off his spectacles, wiped the lenses on his napkin and repositioned them on the tip of his nose. "Absolutely…Canada. Been meaning to move there for years now."

Of course, it was hopeless to protest. Insects had dictated the movements of the Moffat family for as long as James could remember.

His father smiled at him enthusiastically across the table. "You'll go first so you can start at your new school in January. Your mother and I will follow when we wrap things up at the laboratory."

He smiled absently in James' general direction. "There's an incredible *variety* of insects that thrive in the island's cold wet climate and don't forget your cousins on your mother's side. The identification process will be *fascinating*. Why did your mother take the salt?"

James pulled his covers up to his chin. Nobody could complain that life in the Moffat house was boring! Going to Victoria *would* be an adventure; if he was lucky he might finally even get to see snow! He was used to being on his own and besides, going on a steamship up the west coast would be following in the footsteps of the gold seekers. His parents had told him that, only a decade ago, men and women had flocked from San Francisco up the west coast to the Klondike on the heels of thousands of speculators maddened by the gold rush.

Finally, his eyelids began to feel heavy and he drifted back to sleep, sure they were weighted with flakes of snow and gold dust.

With daylight, James' night terror evaporated. The sun poured through his window and he scrambled out of bed and pulled on his lightest wool pants and a casual shirt.

Downstairs on the dining room table, lay a note from his parents scribbled hurriedly on sticky paper. Yuck! They had been handling their specimens again.

The note read:

James, you were in such a sound sleep that we decided not to wake you. I hope you are not coming down with a cold! Take an infusion of camomile tea. Your father is at the laboratory and I am buying you some winter clothing for the journey. See you at lunch.

Love, Mum and Dad

He wolfed down a bowl of porridge, but skipped the camomile tea. The newspaper lay on the table so James glanced casually over the headlines:

The San Francisco Chronicle
Tuesday, 16 January, 1906
Minor Tremors Shake Bay Area

Another tremor — well, he hadn't felt it. James read on: *Three minor tremors shook San Francisco and the Bay Area late last night. Although they were mild in nature, doomsayers are warning that a big earthquake is sure to follow. City officials deny any impending danger and warn the citizens of San Francisco not to panic. "It is highly unlikely that these tremors were anything but a freak occurrence," says the mayor.*

James had heard his parents talking about earthquakes. He had also heard them talking about the mayor. They thought he was fool. He put down the newspaper, suddenly relieved they would be leaving California.

The ship that was to take him to Victoria would be leaving on the 20th of January. That gave him only four more days to prepare — not that he had a lot left to do. All his goodbyes had been said at school on Friday; his clothes were more or less organized. His mother had helped him pack, but, of course, he would have to double-check because she would surely forget things.

James spent the morning in his parents' library reading everything he could about Canada's west — especially stories about the gold rush. He learned that with the *discovery* of gold in the Klondike in 1896, San Francisco had mushroomed into the largest port in North America. It had become the departure city for fortune hunters heading north to Alaska and the Yukon. They took with them nothing more than their stake and a prayer.

The gold rush trickled out, but the shipping industry continued to grow. Ships of all sizes and description plied their trade up and down the west coast, going from San Francisco to Victoria to Seattle and finally up to Alaska. They carried food, clothing, building supplies, dogs, horses, lumber, coal and, of course, passengers.

The more James read, the more excited he became about the trip he was about to embark upon. He was bursting with questions when his parents finally returned for lunch.

"What's the name of the ship?" he asked, accosting them as they stumbled through the door laden with packages.

"Oh good," his mother said. "We were just talking about lunch and wondered where you got to. What ship is that, dear?"

"I didn't *get to* anywhere," James replied. "I was in the library. Anyway, you know, the ship I am sailing on to Victoria."

His parents collapsed at the dining room table and began spreading out before them, on plain white paper, their specimens — long, smooth bug bodies and lacy winged creatures that still looked half alive.

His father's head was bent over the bugs. A small patch of thin hair at the crown of his otherwise bald head flopped forward as he looked up and adjusted his spectacles. "You're back," he said.

"No. *You're* back," said James, frowning and feeling unusually impatient with his absent-minded parents. "I *said* I was in the library."

"The name of the boat starts with a *V*," said his mother. "I think it's a Spanish name. Pass me the tweezers."

"The *Valencia*," said his dad slowly, making the *C* sound like an *S*. A beautiful old steamship — she has been ploughing the waves for nearly 24 years."

"What a pretty name," said his mother. "It's a wonder no one has used it as the common name of an insect. Darn. I've gone and pulled the wing off." She reached for a smaller pair of tweezers. "These will do the job, now if I can just...."

James sighed. Getting information from his parents was always this hard. But he refused to give up. "How big is it?"

"*She*," interjected his father. "Ships are always referred to in the feminine. She was built in Philadelphia in 1882, originally for the Pacific Steamship Whaling Company. She is a two-masted, iron, three-deck passenger steamer weighing 1,600 tons. She is 253 feet long and it takes more than 60 men to keep her afloat. The *Valencia* is a fine ship. I rather envy you."

"Sixteen hundred tons," James breathed. "I guess a steamer that big has to be safe."

His mother looked up from her work. "Your new clothes are in the front hall. I bought you a heavy woollen overcoat, a pair of warm boots, woolly socks, as well as long underwear and a thick undershirt. I think I will only send one trunk with you and the rest of the luggage can come later, with us. It gets awfully cold in Canada this time of year, though the west coast is naturally warmer and wetter."

"Will there be snow?" James demanded.

"It's rare, but possible. Of course there *is* snow in the mountains," his father replied.

"Will there be other kids on the *Valencia* sailing without their parents?" He pulled nervously at a loose thread on his pants.

"I suppose so," said his mother. "There'll be all sorts of people going to all sorts of places."

"What sorts of people going where?" James persisted.

"A ship the size of the *Valencia* will carry more than a 100 passengers," said his dad, "from all walks of life. There will be rich men, poor men, beggar men and thieves."

James' mother frowned at her husband. "*And* women. Besides, I'm sure there will not be any *thieves* on board. But, just in case you should meet any, be careful and keep your wits about you. Anyway, I am sure there will be other children on the ship."

"I don't know," said his father. "Some people *never* go anywhere. They get *stuck* in the present."

"How long will it take to get to Victoria?" James asked, aware that there was never any danger of *his* family getting stuck. They were all over the place.

"Three days. It is not a long voyage compared to some that keep passengers at sea for months on end. You leave here at eleven o'clock on the morning of the 20th and you should be in Victoria by Tuesday the 23rd. The *Valencia* will continue on to Seattle and then up to Anchorage, Alaska," James' father answered, rising from his chair.

"Does the steamship take cars too?" James asked. Their new Ford was his father's pride; most people still used horse-and-buggy to get around.

His father was momentarily disconcerted. "No. I hadn't thought of that," he said. "It can't go with us. What a pity."

He rose from his chair, adjusted his glasses, kissed his wife on the head, tousled James' hair and left the room.

Only after the front door slammed did James' mother ask, "Where has your father disappeared to now? I can't find my slide."

James sighed. There was so much more that he wanted to know, so many unanswered questions, but he knew better than to try to get any information from his mother when her mind was on work.

The clothes she had purchased earlier were in a heap in the entrance way. He lugged them upstairs and dumped them in the middle of his bedroom floor.

He opened his wooden toy trunk and sorted carefully through his belongings. Most of his treasures would follow him to Victoria later.

His tin boats and a replica of the Wright Brother's flying machine would have to wait. After much debate, he finally decided to take his home-made slingshot, his copy of *Moby Dick*, and a real gold nugget — a gift from his parents this Christmas. He added them to the growing pile.

He still wasn't sure which of his things would be coming to Canada with him and what would have to be sold. Of course, all the specimens would be shipped — his parents would see to that. He was nervous leaving his parents to pack up the house. Anything without wings and multiple legs could easily be overlooked. Perhaps he'd better make a list.

That night, before going to sleep, James conjured up the route the *Valencia* would follow, steaming up the coast of California, past Oregon and Washington and finally into British Columbia. He rolled the exciting names around on his tongue — Cape Mendocino, Cape Blanco, Cape Disappointment, Umatilla Light, Cape Flattery, the Strait of Juan de Fuca. His eyelids closed heavily.

James crouched on a narrow bunk in utter darkness.

The steadily rising water sloshed against the walls of his cabin, burying forever everything he owned under its cool, green surface. All around him men, women and children cried out for mercy, while the doomed ship rattled and groaned beneath them. Deep under the ocean, the earth shook and San Francisco collapsed under millions of tons of red hot lava. The quake awoke a sleeping giant — a 200-foot wave hurtled toward San Francisco, toward his home and his parents.

"No!" James screamed, jolted awake by the panic in his voice.

The next morning the edges of the nightmare had softened, but James still felt uneasy. Luckily, there was much to do. There were tickets to be picked up, telegraphs to be sent, clothes to pack, unpack and repack, papers to be put in order, last-minute goodbyes to be said.

The night before he left — Friday, January 19th — James lay in his four-poster bed for the last time. His trunk was packed and sitting in the front hall, his ticket was secured in the inside pocket of his best wool blazer, his starched white shirt, his necktie, his felt hat and his shiny black shoes were piled neatly on his chair. Tomorrow the *Valencia* would sail.

"Good night James," said his mother and father, pushing up their glasses simultaneously as they ducked into the dim light of the hallway.

"Good night Mum, Dad." He struggled to keep his voice steady.

They backed slowly out of his room and the last

thing he heard before the door closed was his mother's soft voice floating across the room:

> *Good night, sleep tight.*
> *Don't let the bedbugs bite.*
> *You're as snug as a bug in a rug.*

But James was too excited to sleep tight. By the time he finally drifted off to sleep, the sun was just peeking over the tall houses of San Francisco.

One thousand miles north of him, below the waters off Pachena Point, dozens of ship's carcasses swayed gently with the incoming tide. Their bleached bones reached into James' sleep, so that he awoke several times during the night, choking, his lungs filled with the sea.

TWO

The ship was cheered, the harbor cleared,
Merrily did we drop
Below the kirk, below the hill,
Below the lighthouse top.

— SAMUEL TAYLOR COLERIDGE,
"THE RIME OF THE ANCIENT MARINER"

"James T. Moffat! I am not going to call you again! Rise and shine! Hurry up. Breakfast is on the table. You have a long day ahead of you and no time for lollygagging about in bed."

James reluctantly opened his eyes and blinked. The sun, weakened by the heavy early morning fog, filtered through his window and skimmed across his bed. He could smell bacon and eggs cooking in the kitchen downstairs.

Today is the day, he thought, untangling his night-shirt and leaping out of bed. *I dreamed again last night*

— a dark dream, maybe even a warning....

"Coming!" he shouted down to his mother.

He ran to the window and peered outside. San Francisco was up to see him off. Horses, pulling wagon-loads of flour, coffee, tools and other necessities, clip-clopped down the steep hill below his window. In the distance, he heard the screech of the bright red, cable cars climbing the hills of the city, as people hopped on and off at various stops.

James stretched lazily and yawned. From behind, he heard his mother's admonishing voice. "You really don't have time to stare leisurely out the window. And close your mouth. If you stand there with it gaping open, you're going to catch a fly. Put on your clothes and get downstairs. It is already nine o'clock. We have to leave for the pier in a half an hour." She hurriedly left the room, her unusually sharp tone betraying the anxiety she felt about his departure.

James stared at his reflection in the mirror above his dresser. He ran a comb through his unruly hair, flattening it down with his spit.

Quickly he pulled on his coarse woollen pants, his starched shirt, his thick socks and his shiny new shoes. He stuffed his tie into his blazer pocket, feeling the bulge of his steamship ticket against his chest. Finally, he grabbed his hat and tore down to the dining room.

His mother and father sat at the table sipping tea, the morning papers spread out before them. James noticed that the usual clutter of scientific equipment was missing.

"Well, at last, James. There you are," said his father. He sighed and pushed his glasses up his nose. "Your tie belongs around your neck, not in your pocket," he scolded. "Never liked wearing them myself," he added, with a smile.

James pulled his tie out of his pocket and fumbled unsuccessfully with it.

"Gracious, James, you're making a horrible mess of that knot," said his mother. "Hold still a moment and I will tie it for you. Gosh, look at that lovely butterfly on the window." She forgot all about his ungainly knot and rushed to rescue the winged creature.

"I'll do it, son," his father offered. "You can take it off as soon as you board the ship," he added, winking at James.

"Not soon enough," James quipped and stood still while his father expertly fussed with his tie.

By the time he had finished his toast, eggs and tea, his trunk was stowed in the trunk of the Ford and it was time to leave.

James climbed into the back, his mother slipped into the front seat and they waited patiently while his father unbuckled the long-handled crank from the hood and slid the big metal rod into a hole beneath the radiator.

"Everyone ready?" his father called and cranked the handle with all his might. The car sputtered to a start.

"Wonderful! A miracle!" shouted James' mother, clapping her hands.

"Hold on," said his father with glee, leaping into

the car. "We're off!"

The car jumped forward and his father applied the brakes as they pulled onto the steep road behind a horse-drawn milk cart on its delivery route.

"Can't you pass it, Dad?"

"Don't want to risk spooking the old nag. Soon everyone will own an automobile and horses will be relegated to the field," predicted his father.

"I think you're right, dear," replied his mother. She smiled. "I believe anything is possible, but I am quite sure horses will be with us for a long time, even if not on the roads. Although without horses there would be fewer flies."

They turned onto Market Street, swerving to avoid a group of pedestrians crossing the wide main road. Saturday morning was especially busy — the street filled with shoppers, merchants, sightseers and street hawkers. Overtaking a cable car, James swelled with pride when a boy about his age leaned out the window to stare longingly at the Ford.

"She's a beaut," James heard him say. "A real horse-less buggy!"

As they rolled down Market Street, toward the Ferry Building, the crowds grew larger and noisier.

"I'm glad we bought your ticket in advance," said his mother. "I would not relish having to fight our way through this crowd!"

James loved the waterfront. Now he could see the Embarcadero, its long wharves jutting like fingers into the bay.

The early morning fog had all but lifted, offering a clear view of the ocean-going vessels loading and unloading their cargo. The waterfront was a hive of activity. Buggies and the occasional motor car wound their way between horses, carts and wheelbarrows. Sailors, merchants, dock workers and passengers of all ages jostled for a place on the huge wooden piers. Ships, between voyages, rocked gently on the calm harbour water.

James, like his mother, pressed his hanky against his nose, but the smell of sweat, perishables and fumes hung in the air like a foul blanket. Cattle, chickens, pigs and mangy dogs shared the wharves with sleek rats, which slithered through the murky water.

Activity was at a fever pitch. Whistles from arriving and departing ships pierced the thick air. Families and friends called out their goodbyes or waved frantically at their loved ones. People teemed over the docks. Huge crates lined the wharves; trunks piled on trunks waited to be loaded into cargo holds. Half-wild dogs ran among passengers and onlookers. Added to the din were screeching seagulls, wailing babies and the whining voices of rambunctious children. James had never heard such a racket!

He loosened the tie around his damp neck. Most of the men were dressed as he was, wearing black suits, white shirts, waistcoats and bow ties. Many of them sported moustaches. Women struggled to raise their skirt hems above the dirty planks, while fighting to keep their small children in view and out of trouble.

The automobile lurched to a stop and his dad wrestled James' heavy, wooden trunk onto the boardwalk. The label, neatly inscribed in his mother's handwriting read:

> *Property of James T. Moffat*
> *416 Ocean Drive, Victoria*
> *British Columbia, Canada*

Ocean Drive. James suddenly felt uneasy. Goosebumps broke out on his arms and his mind reeled back to last night's fractured dreamscape: *He balanced precariously on the buckled deck of a half-submerged ship. Wave after wave, each one higher and more relentless than the last, crashed onto the slippery deck and threatened to drag him into the wild sea. In front of him, but just out of arm's reach, a boy about his age struggled to keep from sliding off the ship into the foaming waters. Blood-red fireworks danced across the stormy sky. The ominous splintering of wood jerked him to attention and the realization that he might never see his parents again. James tasted salt on his frozen cheeks, but could not determine whether they were his own tears or the stinging ocean spray.*

"Dad," he caught his father's sleeve, "when are you and Mum coming to Victoria?"

His father placed his hand on James' shoulder and bent down so that he was eye level with his son.

"James, you know your mother and I wish we were going with you now, but you have to start at your new school. You have already missed nearly three weeks of the winter term. We will pack up the house and follow you to your Aunt Jessie's as soon as we can. Probably in six weeks."

"Tell me again about Aunt Jessie."

James' mother smiled at the mention of her younger sister. "Aunt Jessie looks just like me," she said, "except her eyes are bluer and her hair is browner. Uncle Peter is Victoria's only doctor. His office is built onto the side of their house and sometimes your cousins, Madeline and Jacob, help him when he is very busy."

"Does he just doctor people?" James loved to hear about his cousins so he asked the same questions over and over again.

"No, sometimes he helps the settlers with a foundered horse or a cow that is having a difficult birth. They have a three-legged dog named Hopper that was run over by a wagon. And that is all I am going to say. You'll meet them soon enough and you can see for yourself."

James smiled, feeling better. He stared into his father's grave eyes, wanting to show him he was not afraid, but still unable to shake his mounting fear.

His dad tousled his hair. "Soon, you will be 14, almost a man. I expect you to act like one. Reassure your mother. I know you will be fine."

"Of course I will, Dad," James agreed. "You can count on me," he added weakly.

"Do be quiet, John," cried his mother. "He is still only a boy." She dropped to her knees and flung her arms around James, engulfing him in a bear hug. Her eyes glistened with tears.

Embarrassed, yet on the verge of tears himself, James pushed her away. "I'll be okay, Mum," he said and squeezed her hand.

"Come on, you two," his father urged. He patted the automobile gently and turned to his family. "James, you carry your cabin bag. Now everybody cheer up. Let's go and find the *Valencia*."

The family wound its way through the throng of people: his father leading, James in the middle and his mother lagging behind.

He was about to embark on a voyage, alone among strangers, that would take him up the wild west coast of Canada to meet the cousins familiar to him only through family stories and letters.

"There she is!" His father stopped in his tracks. "Isn't she a beautiful ship?" he added.

James followed his father's finger. Through the clambering bodies, he was able to make out the sleek lines of a large ship. She sat long and low in the water, weighed down by coal and baggage and passengers and something else he couldn't quite identify. The decks were shiny and white in contrast to the stack and ventilators, which were painted a flat, dreary black.

Already, people lined the decks — some were waving and laughing, others stared solemnly back at the bustling Embarcadero. At the stern of the steamer, the American flag hung limply from a flagpole. Puffs of steam hung over the *Valencia*'s stack and passengers milled about the decks or sat atop the pilothouse.

"She's a fine steamer. The Pacific Coast Steam Company bought her in 1902 and the last four years she has been to Alaska and back dozens of times. You're a lucky lad," his dad added with a hint of envy.

James did not *feel* lucky. *Valencia*, he whispered into the raw morning air. The word dropped from his tongue with a hollow thud and he shivered involuntarily. The soft sounding name swam circles in his head like a hungry shark.

"*Row, row, row your boat,*" he hummed, to distract himself from a growing sense of unease.

"*Gently down the stream,*" he hummed louder. "*Throw your father overboard and listen to him scream.*"

He stood stock still, the silly words repeating in his mind, until only an echo rippled the surface of his thoughts.

Finally, James edged forward until he could see the whole length of the *Valencia* stretched out before him. He counted seven lifeboats, each sporting a board boasting the ship's name and the lifeboat number.

"Come on, James," his father called. "It's time to board the ship."

James shook his head. "I'm not going," he protested, his stomach turning. "I don't want to…I'll go with you in six weeks…. *Pleeease….*"

"Pull yourself together, James!" snapped his father, who glared at him by way of reprimand.

James turned his own pleading eyes on his mother. "Please, listen to me," he begged.

His father gripped him firmly by his shoulders. "No, James, *you* listen to *me*," he said in a cold, flat voice. "I don't know what this is all about, but you are upsetting your mother. The *Valencia* is a sound ship with an experienced crew. In fact, I bet there is no sounder ship in this port today. Now is not the time to get cold feet." More softly, his father added, "Going away by yourself for the first time is never easy, but your mother and I have faith in you."

"Fine," James nodded. He was letting his imagination get the better of him. He reached out and grasped his father's big hand. "I don't know what's the matter with me," he smiled weakly.

He threw his arms around his mother and kissed her warm cheek. "See you in six weeks."

Minutes later, with a heavy heart and a resigned step, James shuffled up the gangway onto the deck of the *Valencia*. All around him, fellow passengers talked and laughed. The deckhands ran fore and aft preparing the liner for her journey. At last, the crew retracted the gangway. In that simple move, they severed all contact with the mainland. The voyage was about to begin! *Toot! Toot! Toot!* The *Valencia* blew her whistle three times, signalling her departure.

A handful of passengers shimmied up the ladder on the forward mast to gain a better view of the receding shore. James hoisted himself up after them. It was easy, just like climbing rope ladders in the park near his home. He settled himself into the thick ropes and searched the crowd frantically for his parents. There they were — his mother holding his father's arm, a brave smile on her face.

"Goodbye," he called out to them.

It was too noisy for his voice to carry, but they saw him. He raised his hand. "Goodbye," he mouthed. A photographer on the dock snapped his picture.

"All aboard that's coming aboard!" sang out a deck-hand.

The bosun shouted orders to the crew. He was in charge of all the ship's rigging and it was his job to oversee the raising and lowering of the anchor. As the fog lifted, the heavily laden steamer eased out of her berth and turned her bow toward the mouth of San Francisco Bay.

James stayed in his perch in the rigging until the shore had all but disappeared along with his earlier, illogical fear. Above him a seagull circled and shrieked, before turning back toward the City of the Golden Gate. James followed the scavenger until it was only a speck in the cloudless sky and the coast of California became a dim shadow on the horizon.

"I'll find out all I can about steamships — especially the *Valencia*," he vowed, remembering one of his mother's favourite expressions: THERE IS NOTHING TO FEAR BUT FEAR ITSELF.

THREE

The Sun now rose upon the right,
Out of the sea came he,
Still hid in mist, and on the left,
Went down into the sea..

— SAMUEL TAYLOR COLERIDGE
"THE RIME OF THE ANCIENT MARINER"

Ship's Bosun Tim McCarthy, a friendly man with a severe part in his hair and a big smile, was just the man to provide James with the information he wanted.

James found him on the hurricane deck, the uppermost deck of the ship and often the last one to remain relatively dry in a storm. Tim McCarthy was deep in conversation with a tattooed deckhand.

"This is the lad who is travelling up to Victoria by himself," Tim McCarthy explained, patting James on the shoulder. "And this is my right-hand man, John Marks."

James flinched as John Marks grasped his out-stretched hand and shook it roughly. "So, you're the boy who didn't want to board at the last minute," he laughed. "Your dad wants us to keep an eye on you." He winked at James and added with a grin, "He's afraid you'll jump ship or something."

Bosun McCarthy guffawed, cleared his throat and spat into the sea. "Nobody wants to end up down there in Davy Jones locker," he said, "not unless they have a death wish."

James lowered his eyes, embarrassed.

"You're not the only one with black thoughts," confided John Marks, hoarsely. "Sam Hancock, our cook, saw a black cat board the ship and now he has the willies. The *Valencia* was rammed in 1903 and Sam thinks she has a structural weakness. Said his right leg wouldn't stop shaking all last night; believes that means there is danger ahead."

"Stupidity," growled Bosun McCarthy. "He's an old man who believes old wives' tales and I don't want him spooking the crew. Sailors are a superstitious bunch, so you both just keep your mouths shut. You hear me?" He spun toward John Marks, his eyes glinting. "I'll deal with Sam."

James quickly changed the subject. "How many people are aboard the *Valencia*?" he asked Bosun McCarthy.

"What do you mean? Passengers or crew?" the swarthy little man replied, the twinkle back in his eyes.

"Both," James answered.

"We've got 99…including 17 women, plus…" he held up his gnarly fingers and did a quick calculation, "six children. That's first- and second-class passengers. Then there's the crew — 65 in all, including officers."

"Sixty-five!"

John Marks laughed. "Landlubber. It takes 65 men and women to sail a ship the size of the *Valencia*. Passengers have to be fed, everything on board has to be shipshape, the crew needs to rest and someone has to keep shovelling coal into the furnaces around the clock."

"Aye, that's a dirty job," said the bosun, "but an important one. Without the stokers, the *Valencia* wouldn't move. Have you ever been in the guts of a ship, young James?"

"No, sir," James replied, "but I know how it works."

The bosun ruffled James' hair and grinned. "I'll just bet you do," he teased, "but you might need a refresher course. I'll take you down to the boiler room when I have the time and introduce you to the lads."

"I could go now!" James said eagerly.

"In good time, in good time. But that is enough of your questions for now. I've a ship to sail, so off you go and stay out of trouble."

James quickly found his own stateroom in the first-class cabins. It was very small. His father would have said: BARELY ENOUGH ROOM TO SWING A CAT.

But at least James had his own commode, or *head*. He would not have to share the facilities with other passengers, as those in the second-class cabins did, nor would he have to sleep in cramped quarters surrounded by strangers.

A steward had deposited his trunk in the middle of the room after boarding. It took up a lot of space, so James pushed it beneath the long narrow bed, to allow him to move around more easily.

The few furnishings were built into the walls so that they wouldn't shift in rough waters. A shallow basin, a small table and two bunks, with four-inch high railings to keep him from rolling out, comprised the sum of his surroundings.

He placed his clothes in the narrow closet and swung himself over the railing onto the hard bed. It was tiny, nothing like his big four-poster bed at home. His arm brushed the thin iron wall. It was ice cold. Only inches separated him from the Pacific Ocean. He listened to the sea lapping against the *Valencia*'s iron hull.

His tie was like a noose around his neck. He clawed it off and threw it to the floor.

Knock! Knock!

James jumped, startled. He hastily kicked his tie under the bed.

"Come in," he yelled, but his mother's words of warning came back to him: *Be very careful about who you talk to on the ship.*

"No. Wait. Who is it?"

"Me," a voice replied. "So you *are* in there?" The door opened, slamming against the wall with a loud bang.

"Hey," James said. "Take it easy on my door. Who are you? What do you want anyway?"

He examined the boy standing in front of him. He had a head of carrot-red hair and pale freckled skin. His blue eyes darted back and forth when he spoke.

"I'm in the stateroom next to yours," the boy replied. "Come on, aren't you going to ask me in?" he added urgently.

"Sure…I guess," agreed James, stepping back to allow his guest to enter his tiny cabin.

The boy leapt forward into the room, pushed the door shut and pressed his ear against it.

"*Shh*," he hissed. "I can hear them." He waited, listening. "There they go. I'm safe now. Can I stay here for a while? I had to escape."

"Escape?" repeated James. "Who are you escaping from?"

"My baby sister, Jenny, and the twins." The red-haired boy flashed James a smile and stuck his hand out. "By the way, I'm Alexander Hamilton, formerly of San Francisco, soon to be of Anchorage, Alaska. Pleased to make your acquaintance."

James laughed, took the boy's outstretched hand and shook it.

"James Moffat, formerly of San Francisco, soon to be of Victoria."

"You're travelling alone, aren't you? Maybe we can pass the time and explore a little. We *have* three days."

"I guess so," agreed James, thinking that his mother would surely approve of this stranger. "You don't sound very American. Where are you from?"

"Well, my parents immigrated here from Scotland

when I was six years old. Now we are moving to Anchorage. My dad is going to be in charge of a school there," he added proudly. "I'm 13 now and they tell me I still have a bit of an accent. How old are you?"

"Thirteen," James replied, "but my birthday is next month."

"The twins were born in February too," said Alexander. "They are going to be six and they are the biggest pests around." He stopped talking and listened. "Good. They didn't follow me."

"I don't have any brothers or sisters," confirmed James, somewhat envious in spite of Alexander's disgust.

"It must be exciting travelling by yourself."

"It's not bad," James lied. "I can pretty much do whatever I want."

"Not me," Alexander shrugged. "I get ignored a lot though. The others take up all of Mum and Dad's energy."

James smiled. "I already met some of the crew and I like them. I want to find out everything I can about the *Valencia*. If you want, we can poke around together."

"OK. I'll just go and let my mother know where I am first. Wait for me here." He turned toward the door and banged into the bed. "Ouch!" he said, rubbing his knee.

James grinned. Alexander was a bit clumsy, but he liked him.

Half an hour later the two boys made their way up onto the deck of the *Valencia*. It was already four o'clock in the afternoon and a chill hung over the calm water.

"If we were on a sailboat, we would be dead in the water," observed Alexander.

James tugged his new overcoat tightly around his body. *Dead in the water,* he repeated silently. He leaned over the rail. The *Valencia* sliced through the grey water at a fast clip, leaving a frothy wake in her path.

"No fear of that," he said. "The steam is motoring us forward faster than I would have thought. San Francisco is far behind us now."

Ahead of them lay the savage currents of the Strait of Juan de Fuca, behind them the City of the Golden Gate. The boys smiled, glad of each other's company. In a surprisingly comfortable silence, they picked their way among the passengers sprawled on the decks of the *Valencia*.

An air of excitement hung over the steamer. First and Second Cabin passengers mingled above deck, huddled together in small groups, playing cards, talking, laughing and filling their lungs with the fresh sea air.

"Is that your mother?" James asked Alexander, pointing to a tall young woman struggling to comfort her crying baby.

"No, I don't know who that is," replied Alexander.

They watched the tired woman pacing back and forth on the deck, her long blue dress skimming the smooth planks. The baby wriggled and squirmed in her arms. She sang to him — her voice strong and clear:

> *Rock-a-bye, baby,*
> *on the tree top;*
> *When the wind blows,*
> *The cradle will rock;*

When the bough breaks,
the cradle will fall,
And down will come baby,
Cradle and all.

"Come on, Alexander," said James abruptly. *And down will come baby, cradle and all.*

"Are you okay?" Alexander asked. "You're as white as a ghost."

"I'm fine. Bosun McCarthy said six children were on board," mused James. "You and I are the oldest; the rest are younger, maybe even babies like that one."

"Yikes," agreed Alexander. "Let's stay out of their way."

Alexander surprised James. He possessed a *Who's Who* knowledge of many of the passengers, knowing them either personally or by reputation.

"My parents know everyone in San Francisco," he bragged. "There is Herman Hoelacher. He is a wine merchant. My dad says he is going up north to close a big business deal." Alexander waved casually in the direction of the well-dressed man, who returned his wave with a smile.

"Who is *that*?" James asked, blushing.

"Her?" replied Alexander. "I thought everyone knew *her*. That's Miss Van Wyck. You know, her brother is Critten Van Wyck, the Sutter Street dentist. *Everyone* goes to him."

"*We* don't," returned James. He wished Alexander wouldn't brag so much.

"Anyway, she was the most popular debutante in

San Francisco at last year's coming out ball. People call her the Belle of Sutter Street." She floated across the deck, her thick black hair piled high on her head, looking at no one, staring straight ahead at an invisible point on the horizon.

"The Van Wycks are snobs, at least that's what my mother says," said Alexander. "All they do is go to tea and walk around with their noses in the air."

Alexander pointed to his mother, off in the corner.

"Who is your mother talking to?"

A pale, sickly looking woman wrapped in a fur coat huddled close to Mrs. Hamilton, as if sharing a secret.

Alexander grinned. "You sure are curious."

"My parents keep to themselves. It's insect identification, not human identification that interests them," James giggled. "So who is she?"

"Yikes. That's Mrs. Badescher. She's a hypo...hypo..., well she's always sick anyway."

"Hypochondriac," James interjected.

"Yes, that's it," said Alexander. "Apparently she had a big fight with her husband because he thought there were too many storms at this time of year to travel at sea, but she insisted on going to see her father. He lives in Buckley, Washington. In the end, her husband agreed. Mum said she convinced him it would be the only thing to improve her health."

James spotted their cabin stewardess hurrying along the deck with a tray of cold sandwiches.

"Mrs. Orchard," he called out.

"Hello, boys," she smiled.

Mrs. Orchard was an old hand at working the steamships. "I was on the *Puebla* for years," she had told James earlier, "and I would still be on her if she had not run aground. This is my first time on the *Valencia* — first time for me and a lot of the crew." She smiled. "Now what are you two up to?"

"Just wandering around," said Alexander.

"Well, take care to mind your manners. Remember we don't encourage the First Cabin passengers to mingle very much with the Second Cabins. There's good reason for that," she stated flatly.

"How many passengers are in First Cabin and how many in Second?" James asked.

"Let me see," she paused. "I believe there are 50 in First Cabin and 49 in Second. Some of those in Second are questionable," she said, lowering her voice conspiratorially. "Campbell in Second tells me we have a bank robber on board, running from the law."

"Really!" exclaimed Alexander. "A bank robber on the *Valencia*! Did you hear that James? What's his name?"

"Oh now, I've gone and said something I shouldn't have. You boys just forget it. Men like him are better left alone. I have to get these sandwiches down to Mrs. Callahan. She is in a bad way. Not everyone takes to the sea the way you two do." Mrs. Orchard furrowed her brow and bustled away.

"I wonder which one he is," James said, gazing at the group of second-class passengers engrossed in card games.

"Sooner or later we'll find out," said Alexander confidently.

At six o'clock, precisely, the first-class passengers gathered for dinner in the main salon.

"Thank you for asking me to dine with you," James said to Mr. Hamilton.

"What an elegant room!" exclaimed Mrs. Hamilton, admiring the formally set dining tables. "You children will have to be on your best behaviour."

"Yes, ma'am," said James, accepting the menu from a uniformed steward. He studied it closely.

PACIFIC COAST STEAMSHIP COMPANY
VALENCIA
JANUARY 20, 1906
MENU
1. SOUP
Potato Chowder
2. FISH
Boiled Fish and Lemon Butter
3. ENTREES
Roast Mutton   Corned Beef
4. VEGETABLES
Boiled Potatoes   Cabbage
5. ENTREMETS
Pineapple Pudding   Mince Pies
Cheese, Dessert, Coffee

"*Entremets?* What does that mean?" Alexander queried.

"It means 'dessert,' Alexander," explained his father. "Something you might have deduced from studying the menu before asking questions."

"My dad always says: THINK BEFORE YOU SPEAK," James piped in.

"Thanks," Alexander said, rolling his eyes. "What are you going to eat?"

James decided on the potato soup, the roast mutton, boiled potatoes and for dessert — pineapple pudding.

"You have not lost your appetite," Mr. Hamilton teased, "although it appears that more than half of our fellow passengers have."

"The wind has picked up," observed Alexander. "I overhead Mr. Aberg, the purser, say we might be in for some rough seas."

"Well, I suggest you two eat up, especially if you are planning to tour the engine rooms with the bosun."

"Yes, sir," Alexander said.

"Don't shovel your food, dear," said his mother, leaning across the table and popping a spoonful of mush into the baby's mouth. "Twins, sit still! Oh, Alexander, do watch what you are doing. There goes another glass of milk."

James, not accustomed to so much activity at the dinner table, said little during the meal, but enjoyed the noisy bantering.

"Are your meals always like that, Alexander?" James asked after they were excused.

"Oh no," Alexander replied. "At home we are really loud, but Dad warned us to behave in the salon."

James laughed. "Come on. Let's go find Bosun McCarthy."

FOUR

The fair breeze blew, the white foam flew,
The furrow followed free;
We were the first that ever burst
Into that silent sea.

— SAMUEL TAYLOR COLERIDGE,
"THE RIME OF THE ANCIENT MARINER"

Bosun McCarthy kept his promise to James and Alexander and took them below deck to the boiler room. He warned them, saying, "Keep your hands to yourselves."

"You don't have to worry about me," James said.

The bosun glared at Alexander. "Not me either," Alexander stuttered.

"Don't worry, Alexander," James whispered, "the old sea dog's bark is worse than his bite."

The boiler room was housed in the ship's stern, far away from the first-class staterooms, deep in the belly of the *Valencia*. The boys followed the seaman through a door marked: CREW ONLY. Long before they saw the engines, they heard them. Down below, the sound of the wind and the waves disappeared, replaced by the deep rumbling growl of the *Valencia*'s engines vibrating beneath their feet.

"Careful as you go," instructed the bosun, as he disappeared down an opening in the deck.

"Down there?" Alexander peered through the hole in the floor at a steep metal ladder. A waft of hot air brushed past him.

"Heat from the boilers," McCarthy explained.

They descended the steep ladder, the air becoming increasingly thick and hot, McCarthy first, then James. Alexander went last. Twice he stepped on James' head.

"Sorry," he kept repeating. "Sorry."

The heat in the boiler room was suffocating. Even though they shouted, it was nearly impossible to hear each other over the roar and hiss of the steam engines.

"Stokers," Bosun McCarthy gestured toward the men shovelling heaps of coal into the red-hot furnaces.

Except for the whites of their eyes and their yellowed teeth, they were completely black — a thick layer of soot covering their wiry bodies. They shouted back and forth to each other, coughing and spitting continually.

"Those big funnel shapes you saw on deck are cowls. They move with the direction of the wind and ventilate the stoke pit. Even so, the air down here is bad. It's the coal dust that gets them in the end,"

McCarthy shouted above the din. "It's hard on a man's lungs over the years."

Alexander sneezed. James laughed at the sight of him — coal dust coated his fiery red hair and formed a ring around his eyes. "You look like a raccoon," James teased.

The stokers worked in semidarkness. Black streams of sweat rolled down their tired bodies.

"It must be over 100 degrees in here," said James. "I should have left my overcoat in the cabin."

"Hotter than the fires of hell," chortled Bosun McCarthy. He wiped his greasy hand across his brow, leaving a perfect set of fingerprints on his blackened skin. "Now listen up. I'll show you how a steam engine works."

It was a simple system really, James thought, simple yet ingenious. The stokers fed the coal into the huge furnaces. Above the furnaces enormous hoppers of water are heated to the boiling point — 212 degrees Fahrenheit — creating steam.

"We funnel the steam into these pipes," McCarthy explained. "Harness the energy, so to speak. That energy moves the pistons that drive the engines."

"How do you control the speed of the ship?" Alexander asked.

"Depends on the amount of steam released — the more steam, the faster we go. Steam is the future," the bosun added. "Those crazy Wright Brothers have got it all wrong. Why, they fly in a circle for 28 minutes and suddenly the whole world wants to flash across the heavens in flying machines." He laughed. "We ain't birds."

James said nothing. He remembered his father saying the automobile was the future. McCarthy said steam was the future. And somebody, somewhere, had once doubted either would come true, just as the bosun doubted the possibility of flight.

Alexander was fascinated. "This could be the end of sailboats altogether," he said excitedly. "One day I'm going to ride a steam-powered train all the way across the country and back."

Bosun McCarthy listened patiently to all the boys' questions. They had lots of them, and not just about the boilers either.

"Are there enough life jackets for all the passengers and crew?" Alexander asked.

"More than enough, several hundred, in fact. But we won't need those on this voyage." Bosun McCarthy rummaged through his pockets, finally pulling out a scrap of driftwood. "Always touch wood. I ain't superstitious, just careful."

James remembered what he had said to Deckhand John Marks earlier. He believed in omens more than he'd admitted.

"Are the life jackets tule or cork?" James asked.

"Tule," McCarthy replied.

"What's the difference?" Alexander said.

"Money," McCarthy explained. "*Tule*, or reed jackets are made from cattails that grow all the way up the coast. You may have noticed them; cattails thrive in wet areas. They're a lot cheaper than cork. I know what you're going to say, James, but they are perfectly safe unless they get busted up and the water gets into them. Sink like a stone when that happens."

Sink like a stone. James swung around abruptly and banged his head on the low ceiling. "Ouch!"

"Watch yourself. Back we go. It's late, but I have one more thing to show you, above."

They ascended the narrow ladder. McCarthy scrambled ahead of the boys, leaving James stuck behind Alexander, whose progress was slow.

"I thought you two might like to see our charts. I remember how I loved maps as a boy. Captain Johnson is off duty and the first officer won't mind. Just keep quiet, he's a bit of a grouch." Bosun McCarthy led the boys up to the pilothouse.

The *Valencia*'s first officer turned from the window when they entered. "It's blowing hard out there," he said. "I think we might be in for some weather."

"Boys, this is the ship's first officer, Mr. Petterson. Sir, this is Alexander Hamilton and James Moffat. Permission to show them the charts?"

"Go ahead, Bosun," replied the first officer gruffly, "but keep them out of my way."

McCarthy winked at the boys. "Yes, sir," he said.

He unrolled a worn, yellowed chart and placed it, with some difficulty, on the wide table in the middle of the pilothouse. The *Valencia* bounced in the sea and Bosun McCarthy had trouble keeping the map flat.

"There's San Francisco Harbour, shaped like a

horseshoe. This is our route." The bosun ran his crooked finger over the map, tracing the jagged lines marking the rugged coastline and offshore islands.

"It's here at the Umatilla Lighthouse that we jog off into the Strait of Juan de Fuca," he explained, "and then on to Victoria. The mouth of the Strait is narrow, barely 10 miles wide and easy to miss if you don't have your wits about you."

James studied the map carefully. Just north of the entrance to the Strait lay Carmanah Point, beyond that Cape Beale and a little farther north, Pachena Point.

McCarthy stabbed the map at Pachena Point. "Right there is the worst stretch of coastline in the world," he said. "The surf off Pachena Point can pound a boat to pieces in a matter of seconds. Sailors call it 'The Graveyard of the Pacific' and many a ship has met her end there."

"It's creepy," said James. "I'm glad we don't have to sail by there. Why isn't there a lighthouse at Pachena?'

"It's a question of money, as usual. The government is *always* trying to save a nickel."

"Soundings, please," Petterson said.

"One hundred and six fathoms, sir," an invisible voice boomed back through the brass pipe.

"Fine. Thank you," he replied curtly. Turning to McCarthy, he barked, "I think they have seen enough now, Bosun."

"Right, sir," Bosun McCarthy replied.

"Thank you, sir," chorused the boys.

Outside, the air nipped at James' skin. "It's freezing

out here," he said to Alexander, pulling his overcoat back on.

A gust of wind picked up a lone deck chair and sent it flying into the sea.

"Off you go, boys. Any more questions you have will have to wait until tomorrow." McCarthy disappeared into the damp night air.

The evening flew by. James and Alexander crawled all over the *Valencia*, even going so far as to climb into one of the lifeboats — number five. She was secured to the aft, port side of the steamer and it was easy to creep into her without anyone noticing.

"There is something kind of creepy about this lifeboat," James whispered as they climbed out from under its heavy canvas cover.

Alexander lowered himself quickly out of the boat, falling awkwardly to the deck with a crash.

"Shh," ordered James, looking around to make sure no one had seen them.

"Nothing is going to go wrong on this ship," replied Alexander. "Why are you all doom and gloom? It's bad luck."

"If anything happens, promise we'll stay together. In fact, let's make a pact," James insisted.

"All right. Pact."

Alexander spat into the palm of his hand and offered it to James. James spat into his own hand, before taking Alexander's.

As darkness fell, the temperature continued to drop. Many of the passengers withdrew to the salons or to their staterooms. When it was too cold to stay outside anymore, James and Alexander played Crazy Eights in the main salon until Alexander's mother sent them off to bed.

"I wish I could sleep in your cabin," said Alexander.

"Ask your mother. Maybe she'll let you," suggested James.

"I doubt it," said Alexander. "But I'll tap on your door as soon as I wake up in the morning. Good night." The salon door slammed behind him.

James laughed. As if Alexander could just *tap* on anything!

Alone in his stateroom, James undressed quickly and jumped into his bunk. He pulled the heavy woollen blankets over him and buried his head in the covers to keep out the cold. The *Valencia* rolled heavily on the rising ocean. James lay in the inky darkness and listened to the waves pounding against the iron sides of the ship.

Sleep, when it came at last, was fitful. He tossed and turned on the waves of a nightmare: *He sat high in the rigging of a ship, waving madly to his mother and father, but they could not see him. Above him, the air filled with the shrieks of ghostly seagulls careening in a driving gale. In their beaks they carried bits of flesh that did not look animal. One after the other, they dove at him, attacking his bare head, piercing his skin with their sharp talons. He beat one off, only to have another return. Suddenly, with a resounding crack, the mast beneath him snapped in two like a piece of kindling, and he plunged into the churning green ocean. Down he went, deeper and deeper into his watery tomb. Bloated bodies littered the water, their blackened skin wrinkled, their mouths wide with horror.*

"Be brave, son," his father shouted, floating by.

Suddenly James was standing on an isolated beach. Three ships hovered on the horizon. Their crew leaned against the railings laughing and talking while all around them the storm raged on.

"Over here!" James called out to them. "I'm here! On the beach! Help!"

He was drowning again, this time in the sand. The fine grains closed over his head and filled his mouth until he could no longer breathe.

James sat bolt upright in bed, his body — in spite of the cold — drenched in sweat. The *Valencia* rolled wildly and the line between nightmare and reality rocked too.

He groped around for his watch, reading it before he accidentally knocked it to the floor. His fingers brushed over the worn cover of *Moby Dick*. Sleep would be impossible, but he didn't feel like reading. It was just after midnight, Sunday, January 21st. He had been at sea little more than 12 hours. "Feels like 12 months," he muttered. "And now I'm talking to myself."

His mind reeling, he relived the day's events. He thought about all the passengers he had seen and talked to: the lady with her baby and the beautiful Miss Van Wyck, Mrs. Orchard and Mrs. Badescher, Herman Hoelacher, the gruff first officer and the helpful bosun.

Mostly he thought about Alexander and vowed to have him share his stateroom the next night.

Outside, the wind and waves smashed against the *Valencia* and the last of the moonlight disappeared behind a blanket of fog. By morning, it was obvious to the passengers and crew that they were in the grip of a rising storm.

FIVE

My soul, like to a ship in a black storm,
Is driven, I know not wither.

— JOHN WEBSTER, *THE WHITE DEVIL*

For the passengers and crew of the *Valencia*, the second day at sea was only a portent of things to come. It began with a black, ominous sky and a rolling, sloping sea.

Alexander appeared at James' door by ten o'clock. "Why weren't you at breakfast?" he boomed.

"I didn't sleep so well," James replied. He sat up and rubbed his bloodshot eyes. "I didn't fall asleep until dawn. Come on in and don't slam the door!"

"Sorry," said Alexander, banging the door shut behind him. "My father is always saying that to me, too. No one slept well in our stateroom either. Dad was seasick and the baby cried for hours."

"Maybe your mum would let you sleep here tonight," James suggested tentatively.

"Maybe. I'll ask her. I could sleep on the top bunk."

James swung his legs over the edge of the bed. "It *was* rough last night. I think I would have ended up on the floor myself if it weren't for this railing," he laughed.

"Nice pocket watch," Alexander said, retrieving James' watch off the floor.

"Thanks. I got that from my mother and father for my 13th birthday. See, it tells time and that extra hand tells you the date."

"I see," said Alexander. "So today is the 21st."

"Right," replied James.

"You're so lucky to have a stateroom to yourself. Thank goodness I'm all right, or I would be stuck in there with the rest of them throwing up." Alexander clutched his stomach and gagged, imitating his twin sisters. "Yuck," laughed James. "Were there very many people at breakfast?"

"No, the dining salon was practically empty. Mrs. Orchard says most of her passengers are, 'a wee bit green around the gills.' "

"It feels like we're moving very slowly." James stood up and braced himself against the bulkhead for balance.

"It's really foggy outside. You can barely see your own hand in front of your face. I was kind of scared walking to the dining salon on my own."

"I would have come with you. Why didn't you wake me?" James pulled on his shirt, his pants, a sweater and his heavy overcoat.

"I tried," Alexander replied. "I pounded on the door for quite a while before giving up."

James hesitated. Should he tell Alexander about his terrible nightmare?

"Do you ever get nightmares, Alexander?"

"No. But my sisters do.... The twins *are* a nightmare. Why? Do you?"

"I didn't used to...." James shrugged and looked away. "But recently.... Do you think a nightmare might be a warning of things to come?"

"I don't know. I never really thought about it. Why, do you?" Alexander replied.

"I guess not," James answered, turning away. He muttered something under his breath.

"What did you say?" asked Alexander.

Oh, just a little poem my mother likes to repeat: *Things are where things are, and, as fate has willed, so shall they be fullfilled.*"

"Meaning?" Alexander inquired.

"It means we have to accept our destiny and nothing can change it."

"Well, right now our destiny is to go above deck. Are you ready?" Alexander was getting impatient.

James grinned. "Let's go."

The boys struggled across the slick deck to the main salon. Huge, rolling waves, peaking at 25 feet, collided with the *Valencia* head on, but she valiantly struggled to keep her bow into the driving wind. Broadsiding would deal a crippling blow to the 1,600-ton ship. The spray rained down on them, soaking James and Alexander, even though they were exposed for less than a minute.

Breakfast was over, but the ship's cook, Sam, whipped up toast and jam and a mug of tea for James.

"You have a strong stomach, boy," the cook noted with admiration.

"Thank you," said James. "I hear not too many of the passengers were interested in breakfast today."

"It's only the beginning," Sam said ominously. "This storm will ride with us right up the coast. I don't like it. Mark my words, there's trouble ahead." He shuffled back into the galley, shaking his head and wiping his big hands across his grey apron.

Alexander frowned, shifting from foot to foot.

"Don't pay any attention to him, he's just trying to scare us," James said with more confidence than he felt. "Come on. Let's go see if we can find Bosun McCarthy."

Tim McCarthy was on the upper foredeck, just out of reach of the spray, talking to an angry-looking sailor who, in spite of the cold, wore a short-sleeved, open-necked shirt.

They stopped talking as the two boys approached.

"Top of the morning to you young James and bonny Alexander. This is our Chief Engineer, Mr. Wilson."

The man nodded his head in their direction.

"Didn't see you at breakfast, James," McCarthy chortled. "Are you feeling a bit under the weather?"

"No, not seasick, just tired. Why are we going so slowly?"

Mr. Wilson glared at the bosun. "Not slow enough for my liking," he muttered.

Tim McCarthy turned to James. "There is nothing to worry about. We ran into some dense fog around midnight. It got heavier this morning off Cape Mendecino — too heavy for celestial navigation. The *Valencia* can handle these big rollers, but she has to feel her way through this pea soup until it clears. Any slower and the ship would be swept backward with the current." He directed his words to James, but they were obviously meant for the chief engineer.

"How is your family?" he asked Alexander.

"Not too well, sir," Alexander shrugged. "The twins have been throwing up since last night and now my father is unwell."

Bosun McCarthy turned his black eyes on Wilson. "The passengers are edgy and they will get worse the longer we are at sea. Send the chief steward to me. I want to make sure they are being well looked after."

"Aye," answered Wilson and melted into the damp grey air.

"I'm sorry to hear about your family, lad. The storm will pass."

The *Valencia* rolled heavily to port, righted herself, than pitched violently to starboard. James lost his balance and skidded into Alexander.

"Haven't quite found your sea legs, mate?" McCarthy chuckled. "The old gal will pitch and heave, but she's weathered worse than this in her time."

"But I heard you say the captain can't see, that the fog is too heavy for celestial navigation," said James worriedly. Alexander stood behind him silently.

"It's just a storm," Bosun McCarthy assured them both. "It is rare to travel up the coast this time of year without running into some bad weather. By Monday we'll be sailing into the clear again. You mark my words."

"But how do you know where we are?" James persisted. "Are we still off the coast of California?"

"Nope. Not any more. We are just approaching Cape Disappointment off Washington state. If you're concerned about being off course, don't be." He paused, "But if *you're* worried, then the rest of the passengers are, too," he added, more to himself.

"I don't understand," James pushed. "You said celestial navigation was impossible. That means you can't chart by the stars. How do you know where we are?" Growing up under the watchful eyes of two scientists had taught James to question everything.

"Dead reckoning," McCarthy said flatly. "Have you not heard of it?"

"I know what it is," Alexander interjected shakily.

The *Valencia* ploughed into the chop, bucking and rocking over the rough white water.

"What is it?" James asked impatiently, ignoring the fear written in his friend's pale eyes.

"It's a combination of taking an educated guess about where you are and knowing how deep the water is beneath the keel of the ship. The crew...," Alexander trailed off.

"The ship's carpenter," interjected the bosun.

"Okay," Alexander continued. "The ship's carpenter takes measurements...."

"They are called *soundings*," McCarthy interrupted again.

"Okay. The carpenter takes soundings beneath the ship. The captain knows how deep the water should be as he travels up the coast. From the soundings, his knowledge of the area and careful map reading, he can guess whether we are roughly on course."

"You're close, Alex," said the bosun. "The captain also takes into account the wind speed and the speed the ship is moving forward, as well as the currents in the area."

"You're kidding, right? I reckon we will all be dead, if that is our scientific method. What about a lifeboat drill? Aren't you at least supposed to do a lifeboat drill, just in case the captain guesses wrong and we hit something and sink?"

James gasped, a sharp hand digging into his shoulder. Bosun McCarthy swung him around, pulling James so close to him he could feel his hot breath on his face. His eyes were smouldering.

"I don't want anyone on my ship making trouble! Never talk about sinking ships. You're going to put a curse on the *Valencia* and the whole lot of us if you say those kinds of things out loud."

The bosun yanked a piece of smooth driftwood out of his pocket and rapped on it furiously. "Understand me?" he spat.

James shook himself free. An icy lump settled in his stomach.

"Yes...I understand," he stuttered.

Bosun McCarthy turned to leave. "You mark my words," he called over his shoulder. A second later he was gone, lost in the thick fog.

"What got into *him*?" James said, shakily.

"Boy, was he mad," said Alexander. "I thought he was going to make you walk the plank." It was a joke, but neither James nor Alexander cracked a smile.

Out of the fog, a voice hissed, "*Psst*, hey you. *Psst*."

Alexander jumped, crashing into James. "Did you hear that?"

They peered into the thick air. Nothing.

"Sorry," Alexander apologized.

James rubbed his arm where Alexander had fallen into him. "It's okay. It is kind of spooky out here, so dark in the middle of the day."

"*Psst*."

James swung around, finding himself face to face with a short, olive-skinned man, sporting a head of bushy hair and the biggest moustache he had ever seen.

"Hey, don't sneak up on us like that," James yelled.

"Please, you don't scream," the moustached man pleaded. "Don't scream. I not scary. Please excuse English. I now learning for first time."

Alexander edged closer to James. The *Valencia* rolled again, the motion threatening to send them both flying. The moustached man didn't flinch. He waited for the boys to regain their balance before speaking.

"I am Joe," he said, holding out his hand.

When neither of the boys took it, he let it fall. "Joe

Sigalis. Ship Fireman. First job in America," he added proudly. "I overhear conversation with bosun. He worried too or else not so angry. Crew worried."

James stepped forward. He grasped Joe Sigalis' hand, liking him immediately. "What do you mean, *crew worried*?"

"Curse already on *Valencia*. Not your fault."

James and Alexander leaned forward, straining to hear Joe's trembling voice over the wild wind.

"If you need help, Joe help you. Count on Joe," he said.

He vanished into the thick haze.

"Did you see him?" James faced Alexander. "Did you hear what that guy said?"

"Unfortunately, I did," shivered Alexander. "Did you recognize him?"

"I think I have seen him around. I wonder what he meant when he said 'The *Valencia* has a curse on her'?"

"Sailors are all superstitious. My mother told me that."

"I know," replied James. "Let's go back to my cabin. I have a bad feeling about all of this."

Suddenly the *Valencia* dove, skating down the back of a mountainous wave. The boys gripped each other, sliding dangerously into the railing. Alexander smashed his arm on the steel banister and shrieked.

"Come on. We have to get inside," commanded James.

He pulled Alexander to his feet. Unsteadily, they wobbled down the steep stairs. A dim light shone from the smaller salon. The boys ducked inside as rain began pelting the ship.

The passengers in the Second Cabin salon looked up curiously as James and Alexander appeared. The boys stared back at them nervously. They were all men and James guessed that the 10 or 15 women in Second Cabin had remained below, sheltered from the storm and their crude travelling companions.

"Shut the door," a voice grumbled.

"Don't let yourselves be caught with us. You two belong with the toffs next door."

"Ignore them," James whispered to Alexander. "We won't stay here long, just enough to warm up and let the sea calm down."

"My mum will kill me if she catches me in here," said Alexander looking around him, but recognizing no one among the rabble of adventurers and asylum-seekers.

"They're just like us," James said. "They just paid less for their tickets."

James noticed an unshaven man, alone, shuffling a deck of cards slowly from hand to hand. He looked up when the boys walked in and fixed his dark eyes on them, a menacing smile playing on his thin lips.

"I'll bet you anything that is the bank robber," he whispered. "Close your mouth and stop staring. Otherwise he'll know we know who he is."

"But we don't know who he is, not for sure. Anyway, if I were a bank robber and I had all that money, I would travel in First Cabin," said Alexander.

"That would be pretty stupid. The law is probably looking for a wealthy, well-dressed man. He is obviously in disguise. He won't spend a penny of his money until he gets to Canada."

The burly, coarsely-dressed man jumped up from his chair, teetered on his feet and swaggered toward Alexander and James. Both boys froze.

"Out of my way," he roared, covering his mouth with bruised hands.

He pushed by them and tore out the door, his face ashen, his eyes wild.

The Second Cabin steward sighed. "I've never seen a man so sick," he said to no one in particular. "If this storm doesn't pass...."

"I thought...I thought...," Alexander stuttered.

"I know what you thought. I did too. Come on. Let's get out of here. I think we should go back to my state-room."

As the day wound down, the sea grew wilder, the passengers more frightened. By dinner, even the boys had completely lost their appetites. "Just the *thought* of eating makes me feel ill," admitted James.

Alexander constantly checked on his family. Each time he returned, his report worsened.

"Dad is sick, the baby is screaming and the twins are ripping the stateroom apart."

"Ask your mother if you can stay with me tonight," suggested James. "After all, she has enough on her hands without worrying about you."

Mrs. Hamilton agreed. "As long as you both stay in

James' cabin. I don't want you wandering around the ship."

They skipped dinner. Instead they had Mrs. Orchard bring them some bread and milk, all that their stomachs could handle, before climbing into bed. The *Valencia* lurched violently.

"Do you say prayers?" Alexander asked.

"No," replied James, "but I will listen to yours."

Alexander folded his hands together and closed his eyes:

> *Now I lay me down to sleep.*
> *I pray the Lord my Soul to keep.*
> *If I should die, before I wake,*
> *I pray the Lord, my Soul to take.*

"Amen," whispered James. "God bless the *Valencia*."

SIX

When Stately ships are twirled and spun
Like shipping tops and help there's none
And mighty ships ten thousand ton
Go down like lumps of lead.

— RALPH HODGSON, *SONGS OF HONOUR*

By morning, the temperature had dropped to well below freezing. James and Alexander woke early, cold and uncomfortable.

Immediately, Alexander went to check on his family and returned worried and upset.

"The twins can't stop throwing up and the baby is crying. My mother is scared," he said, "and I am too."

James scrambled in his pocket for his watch. It was after eight o'clock, January 22nd.

"Me too, Alexander," James confessed, his mind still fuzzy from the lingering fragments of his nightmare:

He stands spread-eagled on the upper foredeck of the Valencia. The screaming wind claws at him through his thin nightshirt, but he is immune to its frosty touch, his body already numb with cold. Ahead of him, riding the crest of a 35-foot wave, he spies one of the Valencia's lifeboats. The storm drives it away from him, but just before the small craft disappears, he recognizes the pale, frightened faces of Alexander's mother, father, his sister Jenny and the twins. "Where is Alexander?" he calls, but his voice is silenced by the wind.

"I didn't have a good sleep at all. Today is the day we are supposed to arrive in Victoria."

Alexander flopped down beside him on the bottom bunk.

"*Supposed* to arrive?"

"*Will* arrive," James corrected. "It has to be today."

"And if we don't?"

James looked at the floor. "Then I guess it will be the day after."

"You don't sound very convinced. In fact, you sound like you are sure we will never make it as far as Vancouver Island," said Alexander, tersely.

"I don't know. I just have a bad feeling...." James voice trailed off.

"What are you saying?" Alexander asked doubtfully. "No matter what happens, we have our pact. We have to look out for each other. We swore. Do you know something I don't know?"

"No. It's just...I have this dream every so often. I can't explain it, but I had it again last night." James wobbled to his feet and pulled on his clothes. "Can you hear that noise?"

Alexander nodded.

"It's the wind," James said, "the wind screaming."

He inhaled deeply, suddenly dizzy. An image from his dream rushed back to him, threatened to swamp him: splintered wood, crying voices and the inky black sea closing in over his head.

Water, water, everywhere, Nor any drop to drink. James thought of his father's voice, strong and clear, reciting a favourite line from a long-ago poem. In spite of the cold, sweat rolled down the back of James' shirt.

"I don't know what's the matter with me," he snapped. "Come on. I'm going up on deck. You can come, or not. I just want off this steamer."

Alexander followed him out of the stateroom. The hallway was deserted, but through every door seeped the sounds of frightened, ill men, women and children.

Only the crew were visible on deck. The passengers were all below. The angry grey shroud that had hung over the *Valencia* since dawn blinded the steamer while the fierce southwesterly wind threatened to cripple her. The winds blew easily through their thick overcoats, wailed up their sleeves and whistled down their necks. It slithered through their buttonholes. On the back of the wind rode a driving sleet that pricked their faces and hands with the sting of shattered glass on skin. Still, the *Valencia* crawled forward, forcing her way through the mountainous sea that pounded her weary iron sides.

"It's freezing up here," said Alexander through clenched teeth. "We have to get inside."

James peered into the blackness. "It's like my dream."

"What?" The wind snatched Alexander's voice and hurled it into the storm. "What is like your dream?"

"The wind," James retorted. "I dreamt the wind. Look! Here comes Bosun McCarthy and First Officer Petterson."

He grabbed Alexander's arm and pulled him back into the shadows. "Stay quiet. I want to hear what they are saying."

Ruts, deeper than the cracks in the ocean floor, creased the bosun's worried face. Beneath his calm exterior, an immense anger festered, an anger he could not disguise when he spoke to First Officer Petterson.

"I'm telling you, we can't dead reckon our way through gale force winds. The air is thicker than clam chowder. Why aren't we sounding every half hour? I don't care what the captain thinks. We will die out here if you can't make him see reason and this would not be the first ship Captain Johnson has lost."

First Officer Petterson's shoulders slumped. "He swears he knows where we are." He bowed his head to the wind. "I'll keep trying to talk to him," he promised, but he sounded defeated.

"Talk to him," Bosun McCarthy said. "The lives of everyone on this ship depend on what you say."

The two seamen disappeared into the dense fog.

"Did you hear what they were saying?" James demanded, more scared than cold.

"I'm too frozen to eavesdrop," replied Alexander.

"Why is it so important to do soundings? Why does McCarthy want the captain to take soundings on the half hour?" asked James.

"I guess he wants a baseline reading of the depth beneath the ship. Remember that is part of dead reckoning. A lead weight is dropped down to find the bottom. If the depth suddenly changes drastically, they know we are off course so the captain can correct," Alexander explained.

"No wonder the crew is so worried. So why isn't the captain ordering soundings?"

"Maybe he instinctively *knows* where we are," Alexander replied. "He *is* the captain of the *Valencia*. He's been up and down this coast more than we know. Why don't you just let him do his job?"

"Because if I can't see and you can't see, then surely *he* can't see," James retorted. "He's a blind man. Come on, Alexander. I want to see him. I *have* to see him," James said, nervous but determined.

But James was not allowed to see Captain Johnson. The two boys made their way toward the pilothouse, slipping dangerously on the slick, water-drenched decks. Deckhand John Marks was struggling to close the door when Alexander and James arrived. The tattoos on his arms glowed in the weak light.

"Where do you think you're going?" he demanded gruffly.

"We need to speak to Captain Johnson, sir," explained James.

"No, you need to get back down to your stateroom or into one of the salons. This is no place for boys. Have you not noticed we are in the middle of a gale?" he said, gesturing toward the wild ocean swells.

James begged for just a few words with the captain.

Exasperated, John Marks opened the door to the pilothouse. Inside, the boys glimpsed Captain Johnson, First Officer Petterson and Chief Engineer Wilson. Beside them stood a steward, a tray of empty coffee mugs in his hands.

"Walter," John Marks called to the steward, "take these boys away from here. Get them inside, somewhere safe."

Marks turned angrily to James and Alexander. "Either you two do as you are told or I'll put you both into the stoke pit until the storm is over. At least I'll know you won't freeze to death down there."

Reluctantly, they followed the steward to the First Cabin salon. For the rest of the long, uncomfortable day, the *Valencia* groped her way up the coast. Most of the passengers remained in their staterooms, sick and afraid. By four o'clock, a blanket of darkness descended on the ship.

"The weather's getting worse," said Alexander, "and we are barely moving."

The *Valencia* ploughed through monster waves while people gathered inside in small groups, fear written on their faces. The crew tried to reassure them, but they were becoming more and more anxious. It looked as if the cook's superstitious ramblings might come true — the *Valencia* was in serious trouble. Not until a quarter to six did Captain Johnson, finally, order more soundings to be made, but even as the order sang out through the telegraph, many members of the crew were secretly afraid it was already too late.

Below deck in James' stateroom, the boys, ill and afraid, tried their best to distract each other over another game of Crazy Eights. Unable to concentrate, Alexander said aloud what they both were thinking.

"We should have been in Victoria by now," he said, "instead of feeling our way through the darkness in the eye of a storm."

James shuffled the cards and dealt eight to himself and eight to Alexander. Thirty minutes earlier he had passed the same young mother he had seen the first day as she wove her way toward her cabin, cooing softly to her crying baby. It had been just after eight o'clock. Most of the passengers, queasy and nervous, had already retired to the safety of their cabins and sleep.

The young mother had smiled weakly at him. "She's almost asleep," she explained, nodding to her small baby. "I hope this storm will ease up in the next few hours. Good night."

"Good night," replied James.

She hugged her baby close to her and disappeared behind her door. James had stood watching her cabin door long after she was gone.

"Your turn, Alexander," James said.

"No, your turn." Alexander dropped his cards face up on the bed. "You're not concentrating."

"Sorry, I just keep thinking I want to go back to the pilothouse. First Officer Petterson took the bridge from Captain Johnson at eight o'clock. Do you think *he* would let us in?"

"I don't see what good it will do," replied Alexander.

"Neither do I. But I would *feel* better. I can't explain it."

"Your dream?" Alexander sneered.

James ignored the sarcasm in his friend's voice.

"Well, I can't come with you. I promised Mum and Dad I would read to the twins. Dad is too sick to do anything and the baby is fussing."

James studied his friend closely. Large black circles darkened Alexander's eyes and his already pale skin was pallid and grey. The brilliant shine in his eyes had faded to a dull blue.

James slumped. Why did he suddenly feel so responsible for a boy he had met less than 72 hours ago? James stood abruptly and lurched toward the door as the *Valencia* pitched into a trough, her bow scarcely managing to resurface under the crushing weight of hundreds of thousands of tons of water spilling over her decks.

"The pact, our pact, James. We *are* going to look out for each other right?" James could barely hear Alexander above the groaning of the ship and the howling of the wind.

"Right," James replied.

"Cross your heart?"

"Cross my heart." *Hope to die. Stick a needle in my eye.* James smiled weakly. "I'll see you when I get back from the pilothouse."

"I'm off, too." Alexander jumped up and banged his head on the top railing of the bunk. James grinned. He left the cabin, relieved to be on his own.

But when he stepped out into the dark, wet night his position seemed futile. If the captain had not wanted to see him, why would the first officer listen to the ramblings of a 13-year-old boy who had never been to sea before and whose only evidence of disaster was a half-remembered dream?

He felt his way to the pilothouse, stumbling through the raging wind. Hail and freezing rain poured down on him, turning the deck into a deadly ice rink. Several times, he stopped and steadied himself, mortally afraid of being swept into the sea. No one stopped him. The crew were too busy fighting to keep the *Valencia* stable and upwind. She laboured slowly at a painful four knots.

James flung open the door of the pilothouse and, for a moment, basked in the relative warmth inside. First Officer Petterson, a tall foreboding man with dark eyes, betrayed no surprise at James' sudden arrival.

"Are you lost or just a fool to be out wandering on such a filthy night?" he barked.

"Neither, sir," James stuttered. "Or both," he added uncertainly.

Petterson guffawed. "Well, at least you're honest.

Now who are you and what are you doing here?"

"I'm James. James Moffat of San Francisco. We met earlier."

"I remember. You're the boy I've been hearing about from Bosun McCarthy. You've made quite an impression on our bosun, though not necessarily a good one. This is not a great time to visit the pilothouse. Say what you have to say and make it quick."

James swallowed twice. His mouth was as dry as a sandy beach at low tide. What could he possibly say?

"Sir," he began, "I…uh…I just have a really bad feeling about…."

A voice boomed out of the telegraph, cutting James off. "Chief Engineer Wilson here. One hundred thirty-five fathoms, sir." The voice sounded nervous.

"One hundred thirty-five at the bottom?" Petterson inquired.

"Ah…no, sir. That would be 135 and…uh…no bottom."

"Thank you, Wilson." First Officer Petterson looked out the rain-drenched window at the gale raging around them. So much water smeared the thick glass that little could be seen. He feared the window might implode under the constant hammering. Screeching wind whirled around the deck.

Petterson pulled at his thick, black beard reflectively. James watched and waited, saying nothing, quite sure that he had been forgotten.

The *Valencia* heaved to the starboard and Petterson fought to keep her on course, to protect her vulnerable broadside from the oncoming waves. Two deckhands — Lawson and John Marks — slipped into the pilothouse, their clothes completely soaked.

"How bad is it out there?" Petterson asked.

"Bad as it can be, sir. The ocean is angry. The men are scared."

"The captain?"

"In his cabin," John Marks said, fighting to keep his tone neutral.

Petterson picked up the telegraph again. "Wilson. Take soundings every 15 minutes from this point forward. Contact me as soon as there's a change," he ordered. "Should have been done hours ago," he muttered under his breath.

"How many fathoms deep *should* we be?" James asked.

"Twenty-five to 50, unless we're over the valley in the ocean floor that marks the entrance to the Strait of Juan de Fuca. I'm hopeful this is the case."

"And if it's not?" James asked, dreading the answer.

"If it's not, then we may have passed Cape Flattery and missed the entrance to the Strait. If it's not, then we are where no sailor should ever be in gale force winds, although the captain swears we are near the Umatilla Light off the Oregon coast," Petterson said.

"Are you saying we might be in The Graveyard, sir?" asked John Marks.

"The Graveyard?" whispered James.

"Aye, The Graveyard of the Pacific, " the deckhand replied.

"Enough, Marks," snapped the first officer. "Out of here, boy, back to your cabin. Don't worry. I know exactly where we are and by morning we will be in Victoria, even at 3.5 knots. Now get yourself to bed."

He dismissed James with a wave of his hand.

In the cabin, Alexander waited impatiently for James, eager for his news.

"Now all we can do is wait, like everyone else. But keep your clothes on and your life jacket at hand, just in case," James advised.

While James, Alexander and the rest of the souls aboard the *Valencia* drifted in and out of sleep, the brave steamer struggled on in unfriendly waters.

Captain Johnson remained confident that they were on course.

He would pay for the error with his life.

SEVEN

About, about, in reel and rout
The death-fires danced at night;
The water, like a witch's oils,
Burnt green, and blue and white.
— SAMUEL TAYLOR COLERIDGE
"THE RIME OF THE ANCIENT MARINER"

James was imprisoned deep in the well of his own imagination. While his body rested, his conscious mind waded through the murky depths of sleep:

He stands ankle deep on a rocky, windswept beach, so familiar to him that he knows the depth of every cave and the smoothness of every stone, each sharp edge rounded and reshaped by the pounding Pacific.

Inch by inch, as the ebbing tide retreats, the bow of a sunken steamship emerges from her watery grave, into the blustery air. Every 12 hours, the entombed ship is buried and reburied. She never moves from her final resting spot. Two, rusty orange anchors chain her to the ocean bed for eternity.

The steamship is vaguely familiar.

Bull kelp, as thick as his arm, adorns the wreck, leaving only three letters visible, where once her whole name had been painted. A. L. E. Ale. Who is ALE?

The smooth, bottle-brown kelp sways in the shifting water. Back and forth. Back and forth. In and out. Up and down. An age-old rhythm, tied to the moon.

The bottom is uneven. Salt flows into the cracks between James' unprotected toes. They are wrinkled and translucent like the skin of an old, old man. Shy aquatic creatures — octopi, eels, mud sharks, sea anemones, bottom feeders — thrive far below the haunted surface. Some have made their homes in the bodies of sunken ships, others in the hollow eye sockets of human skulls.

A fish darts in and out of the rusted anchor chains that immobilize the ship. It grows bigger, greyer, shark-like. It changes, revealing a terrifying jaw full of pointed teeth.

The sound of something being pierced. Moans. Some-one is calling him. James swims up and out of his dream.

"James! James! What was that noise?" Alexander sobbed, leaping from his bed and landing heavily on James.

"Ouch! Watch out! I had a terrible nightmare. Was it real, that sound?"

Dazed, James sits up in the inky darkness, sweat pouring down his face. *Shipwreck.* He reached blindly for his life jacket at the foot of his bunk, grabbing only a handful of blanket. Another grating screech exploded around them. *She's screaming! The* Valencia *is dying.*

He imagined the razor-sharp rocks of the unseen reef ripping through her iron belly. He clutched his own stomach and moaned.

The passengers on the *Valencia* awoke in terror. Children cried, adults screamed and, overhead, sheet lightning lit the stormy sky.

James looked at his watch to confirm what he already knew — five minutes past midnight, January 22nd.

"What happened?" Alexander untangled himself from James and bounded to the porthole.

"I don't know, but I *do* know we are on the rocks. That ripping sound was coming from the front of the ship. We have to get out of here, now!" James urged, pulling his friend, frozen with fear, over the tilting floor of the stateroom.

James groped in the darkness until he felt the scratchy wool fabric of their overcoats. "Put this on. It's going to be freezing outside. Have you got your life jacket?"

"Here," replied Alexander in a shaky voice.

"Well, put it on too."

James searched until finally his numb fingers felt the outline of his own heavy tule life jacket. He pulled it over his head, angrily brushing tears from his eyes.

"Remember our pact?" he yelled. "We have to stick together. We have to be brave. Hurry! We don't have much time."

The words were barely uttered when the wounded *Valencia* listed badly to starboard and lurched to a full stop. Nobody realized it yet, but she was wedged between two razor-edged boulders. They sliced into her steel hull like a butcher's knife into a side of beef. A stream of icy salt water assaulted her holds. Thunder mocked the stricken ship.

A chorus of screams from below the cabin floor rang through the air. James gagged, remembering the stoke pit. By now, oily black water would be flooding into the gaping hole in the bow of the steamer. The stokers would drown.

"My family," shrieked Alexander, frantically. He barrelled toward the door, the ship's unnatural angle forcing him to his knees.

"We'll find them, Alexander, don't worry!" James wrenched his cabin door open and they fell into the aisle as groups of befuddled, frightened people stumbled in a growing crowd.

Behind the Hamiltons' door, somebody whimpered. Alexander and James dove into the cramped space. Alexander's parents were desperately rushing to dress the children.

"Come on," James urged, fighting back his rising panic.

It was too dark to see anything but shadows. Mr. Hamilton, his head bruised and bleeding from an earlier fall, clutched the twins in his big arms. Mrs. Hamilton sat numbly on the floor, holding the baby tightly. No one was wearing a life jacket.

"Alexander," his mother whispered. "Thank the Lord you are safe."

"None of us are safe," interjected James. "Get your life jackets on and get above deck. We may need to use the lifeboats."

Cabin after cabin, in first and second class, the same pattern was being repeated, as the horrified passengers aboard the *Valencia* fumbled in the dark for clothes and life preservers.

"Everyone on deck," Mrs. Orchard called, running down the narrow aisle, her white nightgown fluttering around her bare ankles. "No time to get dressed. Put your life jackets on over your nightclothes. Now!"

Minutes earlier, in the pilothouse, Captain Johnson had listened in stunned disbelief as his second-in-command roared out the results of the last sounding: "Twenty-four fathoms, sir!"

"In the name of God, where are we? Put her hard to starboard," Captain Johnson had ordered, as the bow of the *Valencia* slid onto the twisted, jagged reef, dragging the sleeping passengers into a living hell.

The *Valencia* ground to a halt.

"Reverse engines," Captain Johnson had hollered into the telegraph, desperate to get the steamer off the merciless rocks.

The *Valencia* fell backward into deeper waters, still afloat, but mortally wounded.

The Hamiltons and James had just reached the upper deck when the *Valencia* skidded back into the frigid sea. James clutched the ice-encrusted railing with one hand and held onto Alexander with the other.

"Hold on," he screamed, fearing they would be driven into the sea or trampled by the hysterical passengers swarming over the deck.

Horrified, the boys watched Alexander's mother, father, Jenny and the twins get swept up in the mob surging toward the lifeboats on the starboard deck. Alexander and James were pulled to port with a team of deckhands hurriedly preparing to lower lifeboats off the *Valencia*. They were helpless to resist the current of panicked passengers, dragging them farther and farther away from Alexander's family. Time was of the essence. They had to trust that the Hamiltons would climb into a boat and join them on shore.

"No," Alexander screamed as James threw his arms around his shocked friend to stop him from following them. "Let me go." He landed a driving punch on James' shoulder. "Let me go. I have to go with them."

James hung onto his friend, the taste of his tears mingling with cold, salty water. "Come on, Alexander. We have to get to the bow of the ship. We'll see them ashore. I'm sure they're safe," James choked.

They were the only two passengers among the crew members frantically scurrying about the deck. Breaker after breaker threatened to swamp the crippled *Valencia* and pull them all into the raging ocean.

"Don't let go of me," James yelled, desperate to make his voice heard over the deafening roar of the wind and the waves.

The *Valencia* balanced precariously on the reef, her

stern gradually settling deeper into the water. The boys waited for the waves to recede, but it was hopeless. If they did not move forward now, they would be washed out to sea. They felt their way blindly toward the bow of the *Valencia*, holding onto each other, and the railing, tightly.

In the pilothouse, the ship's carpenter's voice broke as he informed his captain. "The stokepit is filling with water. There is a huge hole in her bow and the stern is fully submerged."

The *Valencia* heaved backward a few more feet.

"We're going down!" yelled Petterson.

Meanwhile, James and Alexander scrambled toward the bow of the ship. Wave after wave flooded the decks. In minutes, the sea was filled with clothes, dishes and anything that was not secured to the ship.

Instinctively, James dragged Alexander toward the pilothouse. The going was treacherous. The nose of the *Valencia* pointed up and toward the open ocean.

At least she has stopped moving, thought James. *If we don't sink, we might have half a chance at survival.*

"We're going down," James heard Petterson cry as they burst through the door of the pilothouse.

James recognized Captain Johnson, First Officer Petterson, the ship's carpenter and Bosun McCarthy staring out the window into the thick fog.

Suddenly Petterson pointed and everyone followed his trembling finger. Outside, almost hidden by the driving sleet and ocean spray, rose a menacing cliff, straight out of the whirling surf.

"I can see shoreline," Petterson shouted excitedly.

James cheered. It was true! Through the rain-drenched glass, he saw a black shadow. Only a short distance separated them from the safety of land.

Captain Johnson sprang to life. "Full speed ahead," he ordered down the telegraph. "Wilson, get her back on the shoal. I'll not sink her in deep water."

The *Valencia* sprang ahead and ground onto her final resting place with a hideous shudder. A curtain of darkness slowly descended over the steamer as, one by one, the last of her lights extinguished. The small group gathered in the pilothouse held their collective breaths.

Bosun McCarthy was the first to speak. He voiced what they all knew. "That's it," he breathed. "The water in the hold has smothered the engines. It's all dead down there now. The stokers...." He crossed himself silently.

A ghastly certainty entombed the crippled *Valencia*, broken only by the crashing of waves, the wailing southerly wind and the terrified cries of the passengers ringing through the foul night.

"It can't be more than 50 feet from here to the cliffs," said McCarthy finally.

"It may as well be a 100 miles," scoffed Captain Johnson. "This gale is running at more than 60 miles per hour. Did you not see before the lights died that a savage wall of water separates us from salvation?"

"We can't just give up," argued McCarthy, his eyes boring into his captain's. "Not yet, not with all these people aboard. We have to try to get to shore."

"He's right," James said. What was wrong with Captain Johnson? Why did he just stand there? James clenched his fists tightly, afraid he would reach out and shake the paralyzed man.

James glanced out the window again, but now total darkness shrouded the bluffs. Though he could no longer see them, the cliffs *had* to be there. He had seen them rising out of the churning ocean in the *Valencia*'s lights, just before they were extinguished forever.

"We will not give up," stated Petterson. "Not when safety is only spitting distance away." He touched Captain Johnson's arm lightly. "Your orders, sir?"

"Yes. Quite right. Prepare the lifeboats," the captain ordered weakly. Under his breath, in a barely audible voice, he mumbled, "God forgive me."

He pressed his hand against the hard outline of a small handgun bulging in his pocket.

"All hands on deck," Captain Johnson ordered. He repeated his order down the telegraph. His voice was strong, but his heart was broken.

"Where are we, sir?" Petterson asked. "I mean, do we have any idea?"

"I don't know," replied the captain, shaking his head, "but we are not where we should be. I could swear I saw the lights of Umatilla...."

"The north currents are stronger out here — stronger, maybe, than we realized. The Davidson current is unpredictable...." Petterson shrugged.

"Stronger than *I realized*, you mean to say. All right, out we go. It will take all of us to organize the passengers." Stricken, Captain Johnson edged into the bitter cold, the others following him solemnly.

The *Valencia* teetered, but remained impaled on the rocks. On deck, battered by the wind and the sleet, small groups of survivors gathered, cloaked in dread.

Alexander slipped, falling flat on his face. "Ugh… cabbages!" he exclaimed, pulling himself up.

"Cabbages?" James looked down. Alexander was right. The deck was strewn with cabbages. "There must have been crates of them in the cargo hold!"

"We are the only people wearing life jackets," said Alexander, removing a cabbage leaf from his hair. "But it's too far and too cold to swim."

"Remember our pact," James reminded him.

"Too cold for my sisters. They hate being cold." He turned the soggy cabbage leaf distractedly in his hand. "James. They made it to shore, didn't they? My dad and mum are both good swimmers."

James gripped Alexander around the shoulders. "I think they made it to shore and now we have to, too. Fight, Alexander! Stay calm!"

"Load the passengers into the lifeboats. Women and children first. Lower them part way, to the saloon deck and lash them there. The water is too rough and it's too dark. And for God's sake, try to calm them down," shouted the captain above the din.

But it was no use. Sensing terrible disaster, the passengers pushed and shoved their way toward the lifeboats and clambered aboard. Horrified, James watched as people pushed each other overboard in their struggle.

Beside him, Captain Johnson yelled helplessly, "Don't lower the lifeboats! It's too rough. Do not abandon ship! I repeat, *do not abandon ship!*" His desperate plea, scooped by the wind and flung cruelly out to sea, went unheeded.

James grabbed Alexander before he could dash to a lifeboat. "If we have any chance for survival, we have to stay here and listen to the crew. We have to wait until the panic is over."

"But what if she sinks!" Alexander screamed.

"She seems stable," James said hopefully. "If we are lucky, she will stay on the reef until help comes."

"*If* help comes," Alexander cried, turning his back to the wind.

EIGHT

Alone, alone, all, all, alone
Alone on a wide wide sea!
And never a saint took pity on
My soul in agony.

— SAMUEL TAYLOR COLERIDGE
"THE RIME OF THE ANCIENT MARINER"

Help, James guessed, would be hours away. First, some-one employed by the Pacific Coast Steamship Company would report that the *Valencia* was overdue to arrive in Victoria. Telegraphs would need to be sent back and forth; other ships in the area would be notified to watch for the tardy steamer. Family and friends, waiting to meet the *Valencia*'s passengers, would begin to worry. Finally, a full-fledged rescue operation would begin. James just prayed it would arrive in time.

He was glad for his thick overcoat and the heavy tule life jacket bound tightly over top. Around him, many of his fellow passengers shivered in their night-clothes. At least he and Alexander had been cautious enough to go to bed fully dressed. Even so, he was cold, dreadfully cold.

A half-filled lifeboat toppled, bow first, into the choppy sea. Giant waves swirled around the crippled *Valencia* like hungry sharks drawn to the scent of blood.

"Why can't they listen?" James asked, turning helplessly to Alexander. "Don't they see that the more they panic, the quicker they'll die?"

Lifeboat number six, three-quarters full, broke away from the *Valencia* and plunged upside down, spilling her passengers into the hungry Pacific below.

Three more lifeboats were launched. James and Alexander watched helplessly as men, women and children, mortally terrified, pushed past the frustrated crew and hurdled into the wildly careening lifeboats. Within minutes, most were swallowed by the sea.

Captain Johnson, Bosun McCarthy and the crew continued to hurl orders: "Please stay calm. Don't panic. Do not lower the lifeboats. Do not abandon ship," but few people paid them any attention.

When lifeboat number four, filled to only half her capacity, was launched into the darkness, everyone remaining on the *Valencia* held their breath.

"I believe she might make it," someone spoke up.

The boat climbed the back of the first massive wave and disappeared into the foggy, black night.

"No way of knowing if she made it until daylight, but pray to God she did," Petterson said.

"I'm not getting in a lifeboat," swore Alexander. "It's safer here."

"You've got your head on straight boy, but those folks haven't kept their wits," McCarthy said, overhearing Alexander. "Move higher, to the hurricane deck," he ordered.

Subdued but terrified, the remaining passengers shuffled forward to the hurricane deck. Less than half an hour had passed since the ship had run aground, and six of the *Valencia's* seven lifeboats had already been launched, as well as three life rafts. Nobody wanted to try their luck on the remaining boat. They had seen enough.

The young woman with the tiny baby brushed by James as she picked her way to the hurricane deck. She clutched her child close to her body. Behind her, also in an ankle-length nightgown, followed poor Mrs. Badescher, who, for once in her life, really *did* have something to complain about. Miss Van Wyck trailed behind, crying.

"I would put that lifejacket on if I were you," advised Mrs. Orchard kindly.

Miss Van Wyck hurriedly pulled her life jacket over her head. "Are we going to be rescued? Will we have to go ashore in a lifeboat?"

"Just follow the captain's orders and I'm sure help will come very soon," Mrs. Orchard assured her.

"What are we going to do, James?" Alexander asked, waiting uncertainly for James to make a move.

"I'm thinking," James replied. "The captain said the

Valencia won't break up tonight. He has no reason to lie to us. I don't like being stranded out here, but there is nothing we can do. At least not until morning." *If we survive the night.*

James squinted into the driving sleet and pushed his cold hand out in front of him. "I can't even see two feet in front of me."

"Come on, Alexander," he took his arm gently. "Follow me."

When Alexander hesitated, James pulled him along beside him. "Alex, one of my mum's favourite stories is about a delicate butterfly. I wish I could remember its name. Anyway, it flies 6,000 miles on its own, from north to south in search of food. I asked her once how it knew where it was going and you know what she said?"

Alexander shook his head.

"She said living things have an enormous instinct for survival, stronger than anything else on Earth. Alex, your family has that same instinct. We have it. The trick is to trust it."

They joined the line of passengers at the end of the slippery deck. Behind them, the ocean hissed, lapping at their feet. The stern of the *Valencia* was now totally submerged in the sea and the nose of the once-proud steamer pointed heavenward.

"Move along, lads," McCarthy advised kindly. "It is still dry at this end. The pantry is above water and the stewards are going to bring out food. We will be safe until daylight."

James smiled weakly at him. Daylight — more than five hours away, five hours outdoors in a driving gale.

The stewards gave portions of soggy bread, corned beef and cold tea to the remaining 115 passengers and crew. They ate quietly, bracing themselves for the long night ahead.

"If we are not smashed to pieces on the rocks, we will freeze to death," cried Alexander.

"Think how *they* feel." James gestured toward the others. "Most of them have only their life jackets to protect them from the biting cold."

Once everybody had finished eating, the captain spoke. "I thank you all for your cooperation *Valencia* passengers! Tomorrow, with daylight, we will find ourselves in a much better position for rescue. At daybreak, we will attempt to shoot safety lines to the shore, using the grappling gun. Meanwhile, the crew and I will fire flares throughout the night, to alert any passing ships to our plight. The *Valencia* is stable. We have food. Every one of you should have your lifejacket on and, God willing, we will be on dry land tomorrow."

Everyone strained to hear Captain Johnson's words above the screaming wind. It was too much to hope for, but it was all they had in the absence of other reassurances — from nature or from any rescuers.

They tried to rest and to conserve their energy. The cold was the worst, that and the terrible symphony of wind and waves that muted their sobs. They rubbed their hands together, slapped their thighs and huddled in small groups, hugging each other for warmth, but their efforts were no match for the terrible force of the raging storm.

Some passengers, 20 or more, scaled the ratlines, climbing as high up the mast as possible and lashing themselves to the rigging, fearing the freezing water lapping over the lower decks more than they feared the driving wind swirling about the *Valencia*. Still, the majority of the passengers spent the long night huddled together on the small deck, praying and crying.

James drifted in and out of a waking and sleeping nightmare, unable to tell one from the other. Beside him, Alexander wept silently, before falling into an exhausted sleep.

Dawn arrived on the wings of the storm. It was howling and screeching and ugly.

"It was better in the dark," Alexander sighed to James as they gazed toward the fractured shoreline. "At least then we could pretend rescue was possible."

Not even Captain Johnson could disguise his dismay as he stared out at the rolling, churning bank of water that lay between the *Valencia* and the lofty, rugged cliffs guarding the shoreline.

"Even if we get to shore, I have my doubts about tackling those cliffs," the cook muttered as he handed out morning rations.

"Is there any chance that some of the passengers made it to shore last night?" James turned to ask John Marks quietly, gratefully accepting a piece of rain-soaked bread and a pickled egg from the cook.

"Aye. There is always a chance, lad." Captain

Johnson prepared to speak again.

"I hope he is not as worried as he looks," grumbled Alexander.

"John Marks thinks it very likely that those who left on the lifeboats last night made it ashore," James exaggerated.

"Good," replied Alex. "Very good."

James stopped chewing and strained to hear the captain's words.

"We have survived the night. My hope is that somebody made it to shore last evening, or our flares were spotted during the night and that, even now, rescuers are steaming toward us. We all need to remain calm. My crew will attempt to fire safety lines from the steamer to the cliffs yonder. Once we anchor a line to firm ground, a bosun's chair will be suspended from the rope to the cliffs and you will be able to ride safely over the surf to land."

The captain stepped aside to whisper something to his first officer.

"Sir, do we have any idea where we are? Are we at all close to a town or a village or a lighthouse?"

"No, Petterson. I regret to say we are completely lost."

"With respect, sir, the chances of the line piercing the ground, without someone to secure it ashore, are almost nil. There is nothing for the harpoon to snag onto anywhere on those cliffs, even if it does chance to reach that far."

"Correct, Petterson. But do you have a better suggestion?"

"No, *sir.*"

James only caught a snippet of the conversation between Captain Johnson and First Officer Petterson, but it was enough.

Chances...almost nil. James felt sick.

The crew were hard at work preparing the safety lines. First, they fastened a large harpoon to the end of a rope. A grappling gun would be used to fire the rope toward land. They hoped that the harpoon, acting as a giant hook, would grasp something solid ashore, forming a kind of rope bridge between ship and land. If that worked, the passengers could be relayed to land in the bosun's chair, a small, triangular seat that is normally used to scale the masts.

"I hope they know what they're doing," James said to Alexander, reluctant to share the details of the overheard conversation lest it further panic his distraught friend.

"Seems like a long shot to me," he replied.

"It's a shot at least. There *is* hope. Please don't give up, Alexander."

As the morning wore on and the weather worsened, their hopes dwindled. The captain fired line after line toward the hostile shore, into the driving rain and sleet. Again and again the harpoons bounced off the hard rocks and into the ocean.

"Our only chance is to secure the lines on shore," said Chief Engineer Wilson.

"I think the lines are falling short of the target anyway," observed Deckhand Marks.

A flash of fire lit the deck. Captain Johnson doubled over, screaming in pain.

"The grappling gun misfired!" yelled McCarthy. He bent over the captain. "God help him!"

"What is it?" Petterson asked.

"Two of his fingers are gone, blown away!" Bosun McCarthy had turned a chalky white.

The cook rushed forward and pressed a damp towel against the captain's bloodied fingers. "Wrap your hand, sir. You're losing blood."

Captain Johnson took the towel. "Don't mind my fingers! Away with you," he snarled, binding his hand in the towel. "The grappling gun is destroyed. Someone must swim to shore." He spoke through his pain, his teeth clenched, his red, broken hand clenched to his heart.

"Who among you will volunteer?"

"Is he crazy?" someone muttered. "Who could swim in *that*? Six lifeboats didn't make it through that wall of water."

A small man with a big moustache stepped forward and raised his hand. "I do it, Captain. You count on Joe."

"Look, Alexander," said James. "It's Joe Sigalis!"

Joe stepped proudly through a crowd of his fellow shipmates. They pounded him on the back and shook his hand.

"Good for you, Joe," they called out.

Joe beamed. He took the thick line from the first officer and tied it around his waist. "May God be with me," he said and disappeared over the side of the *Valencia*.

James, Alexander and everyone on board watched despairingly as Joe made repeated attempts to reach the shore, but the mighty ocean was too great a rival for him. Twice, he narrowly missed being dashed to pieces on the rocks. Valiantly, he tried again, but it was no use.

"Bring him aboard," ordered Captain Johnson finally.

"Even if he didn't make it, he is the bravest man I know," James said.

The crew hauled Joe out of the water. He was shivering, exhausted and barely breathing. They wrapped him in damp blankets, as there were no dry ones left.

"I so sorry," he muttered through blue lips. "I so sorry."

Suddenly, the *Valencia* groaned. Her decks creaked. She shifted violently, slipping back a few more feet into the wretched water.

Screaming, Alexander threw himself onto James. "I don't want to drown!" he cried.

"Move forward! Everyone forward! Now!"

The crew hustled the terrified passengers forward to the only remaining dry area on the steamship. As they swarmed toward the bow, the hurling waves surged over the badly listing *Valencia* and came dangerously close to James and Alexander. Thirty unlucky souls, huddled too close to the rail, were swept into the sea.

"The bank robber is gone," said Alexander. "They are all gone."

"There's hardly enough room for all of us here." James squeezed over to make room for Miss Van Wyck.

"I'm not staying," she replied. "I'm going up there." She pointed to a clutch of 20 or more passengers scrambling up one of the masts. "I want to be as far away from the sea as possible," she cried, as she joined the others making their way up the pole.

The mast was slick and wet, bent with the weight of too many people. James looked up. Miss Van Wyck was near the top. Her hair lashed about in the gale.

Suddenly, a terrible splintering sound rocked the *Valencia*. The mast snapped in two like a brittle matchstick, teetered for a moment in the wind and then, with a thunderous crack, lunged into the ocean.

NINE

Me thoughts I saw a thousand fearful wracks;
A thousand men that fishes 'gnawed upon;
Wedges of gold, great anchors, heaps of pearl,
Inestimable stones, unvaluèd jewels,
All scatt'red in the bottom of the sea.

— SHAKESPEARE, *RICHARD III*, ACT I, SCENE IV, 24–28

As the day advanced, the grey light filtered through the storm clouds exposing the hopelessness of the *Valencia* in all its naked agony. For the first time James realized that he might not leave the *Valencia* alive.

The ocean claimed the condemned steamer, inch by inch. By mid-afternoon, the passengers and crew were forced to retreat to the saloon deck, an area so small they were squashed together like a colony of mussels.

In spite of the disastrous splintering of one of the two masts only hours earlier, the few surviving women, numb with cold and shock, climbed into the rigging, some clinging to children. The spray, even at that height, washed over them, stinging their cold skin. Fine icicles were woven into the women's long hair and into the beards of fathers and husbands.

James, numb and exhausted, barely flinched as the *Valencia* surrendered to the gale bit by bit, settling even deeper into the Pacific's unforgiving waters.

"If we are out here very much longer, we will die from exposure," Alexander warned.

Captain Johnson stepped forward. His uniform hung off him, torn and drenched. The blood-soaked towel covering his mangled hand shook uncontrollably. He spoke forcefully, pain beneath each word.

"We have only one lifeboat left," he began. "It will carry eight, maybe nine people. I beg that the women and children abandon ship. Bosun McCarthy, along with an able-bodied crew, will attempt to reach the shoreline. It may be your last chance. Please come down from the rigging and step forward. There is no time for delay."

Nobody moved. They feared leaving the relative safety of the *Valencia*. All of them had seen the fate that had greeted the passengers the night before. James and Alexander still held out hope that the lifeboat carrying the Hamiltons had miraculously made it ashore.

"Don't be governed by your fear," pleaded the captain, scanning the decks for volunteers.

James made his decision. "I'll go! I'll go and so will my friend." He pushed Alexander forward and stepped forward himself.

Bosun McCarthy smiled at him. "Good lad. You're brave boys."

James took one lingering look at the people he was leaving behind. The young woman with the infant, like most of them, had stubbornly refused to go in the lifeboat. Instead, she had chosen to remain behind and take her chances perched in the swaying mast.

James thought his parents would have said the women resembled butterflies, drifting high in the sky. Their thin clothes blew about their cold bodies and their hair whipped around their pale faces. As he headed toward the lifeboat, the clear, high notes of a gentle hymn rang in his ears.

A *choir of angels*, he thought sadly, turning to look at them once more.

"Who else?" the captain called. "Anyone else?" Five men stepped forward, followed by two others.

Behind James a gruff voice bellowed out, "I'll not step foot in one of those boats, but I'll make it worth someone's while if they guarantee my survival. All he has to do is get help fast, to get me off this bucket of bolts."

The speaker, an overweight man with a ruddy complexion, was the first-class passenger returning to his gold mine in Alaska. Pushing through the crowd, he grabbed James roughly by the collar and thrust a heavy canvas sack into his hand.

"There is more than $1,800 in gold in this sack. It could all be yours. All of it." He took back the sack quickly and stuffed it into his own jacket "Find help. If I get off this death ship alive, you will be the benefactor. Remember, tell the rescue party I will make them rich."

McCarthy stepped between the man and the boy. "All our lives are of equal value," he said angrily. "Now, either you're coming with us or you wait here. No deals. I'll not bargain with a coward and neither will the lad."

Another enormous wave swept over the listing *Valencia*. The captain shook his head sadly. "Any more volunteers? Any other passengers willing to ride in the lifeboat?" He looked up beseechingly at the desperate souls dangling in the wind above his head. They continued to sing.

"All right, then. The rest of the boat will be filled with crew members. We have little time to lose. Listen carefully, Bosun. *When* you get to the shore, climb the cliffs immediately. I will try to fire a lifeline to you. We will work on repairing the grappling gun. If you can, secure the line. Once the line is secured we will begin transferring the passengers." He gripped the bosun's shoulder. "Godspeed."

One by one, they manoeuvred into the swinging lifeboat.

"Come on, Alexander." James held out his hand and guided Alexander into the hard seat beside him. "This is our last chance."

Joe Sigalis positioned himself in front of the two boys. "I'm glad he's here," said James.

It seemed to take forever for everyone to settle in the boat. At last they were all ready. From the deck, Captain Johnson studied the waves carefully before signalling to lower the lifeboat into the madly foaming sea. For a long moment, the little boat swayed dangerously, crashing into the iron sides of the *Valencia*.

"Cut the lines," the captain ordered.

The lifeboat dropped heavily into the pitching grey-green sea and a second later she was swallowed in the thick fog. The small boat climbed and dove in the giant, rolling waves. James and Alexander clutched each other and the side of the boat, while the crew fought to keep it from smashing into the partially-hidden rocks.

Joe was the first to lose his oar. It shattered in his hands, sending him spilling backward into the bilge. He pulled himself back into the lifeboat and continued rowing with the oar's broken handle. John Marks' oar split in his hands, leaving him with only his voice to encourage his mates' slow progress through the storm.

"James! James! I'm so *scared*!" Alexander sobbed.

Giant waves hurled into them, driving the lifeboat sideways toward the lethal rocks.

"Alexander, if we go over, you have to hold on to me. Don't let go! We can't get separated. Alexander, do you understand?"

Even though the rough shore lay only 50 feet from their lifeboat, for five hours they battled the raging surf. They were near death when a mountainous wave slammed into the lifeboat, sending it flying end over end into the rolling swells. The icy water engulfed them. Salt water filled James' eyes, nose and mouth, choking the life out of him.

Don't let go of Alexander, his mind screamed.

Cross my heart. Hope to die....
Which way was up? Which down?
Have to get to the surface! Have to breathe, he told himself, repeating it over and over again. But his lungs were on fire. He opened his mouth and broke the surface, gulping in a lung full of air! He was alive!

In front of him, a lifeless body drifted haphazardly toward the sneering rocks.

Not going to happen to us, he swore silently. Alexander was beside him, coughing, but afloat.

Half dragging his friend, James kicked through the waves, groping his way blindly to the rocky beach and the cliffs that he knew lay just ahead. He had no strength left in him. He had lost his shoes in the swim. Now, something sharp sliced into the soft skin on the soles of his feet. Barnacles! Shore! A fat green piece of bull kelp wrapped around his ankle, threatening to drag him back out to sea. Alexander slipped out of his hands, but only for a second. James reached into the salty water and towed him toward firmer ground.

"You can't have him!" James screamed angrily at the sea. He pulled Alexander safely ashore and collapsed beside him.

"Alexander. We made it. Land. We are alive!" He shook Alexander. No response! "Don't give up," he pleaded, pumping his friend's waterlogged chest, the way his parent's had instructed.

Alexander sputtered and coughed. James rolled him over onto his side and thumped his back. Alexander spewed a stream of salty water.

For a long time after that, James remembered nothing. He fell into a delirious sleep, drifting in and out of consciousness on the rocks of Pachena Point. When he awoke, someone was shaking him.

"Wake up, James." A cold hand slapped his frozen cheek. "Come on, we have to go."

James opened his eyes. It was almost dark. He was freezing cold. Alexander leaned over him. He sat up. "You're still here," he said, grinning.

He blinked. Streaks of fire arced across the black, rain-filled sky. On board the *Valencia*, Captain Johnson was shooting flares into the weak afternoon sky. The rescue ships had not yet come.

Alexander leaned down and helped James to his feet. "Okay. I've done a little exploring. We'll cross the beach, climb over that bank and scale the cliffs just beyond it," Alexander said, suddenly in charge, though clearly still in shock. He planned to launch a search for his family on shore.

He set off at a good pace, carrying only the sail from the lifeboat that had washed ashore, empty. "We might need this to double as a blanket," he explained to James.

James followed stiffly behind him, unable to speak, each step an effort. They stuck close together, scrambling over the rocky bank, where a wall of trees confronted them. Alexander spotted a narrow, roughly hewn trail, barely discernible through the dense underbrush.

"Telegraph lines!" shouted Alexander, pointing to the huge trees, where cables had been snaked through the branches at the height of a grown man.

"That means we are close," said James.

"Closer than we imagined. Look." Alexander pointed to a wind-battered sign nailed to an old cedar: THREE MILES TO CAPE BEALE. "It must be a lighthouse."

"It is," said James, grateful for the time he had spent pouring over maps at home in San Francisco. "It's the Beale Light! We are on Vancouver Island, but way off course!"

"We'll have to follow this trail to help."

"But Captain Johnson said we were to go straight to the cliffs to secure the lines from the *Valencia*." James faced Alexander squarely. "He ordered us to do that. Those people are counting on us."

"He gave his orders without knowing we were so close to Cape Beale, without even knowing we were on Vancouver Island! There is a lighthouse keeper stationed at Beale. I remember seeing it on the map that day. He will have a telegraph and supplies."

Alexander started up the tangled trail. It was little more than a footpath carved through the forest. James followed him, his head bowed against the driving wind.

Alexander stopped to wait for him. "What are we going to do, then?" Alexander whispered through cracked, frostbitten lips.

James shivered. His fingers and toes had long since stopped hurting. Now, he could hardly feel them. He had read about people who had died of exposure. First, they lost the feeling in their bodies, then their judgement. James knew if he and Alexander died out here, they could not help the others. He made a decision. "We go to Cape Beale."

Once off the stormy beach, the shadow of the trees blocked all light. Alexander picked his way through the dense underbrush along the narrow track that hugged the cliff face. The thorny nettles cut into James' feet. He winced with each step.

Lighthouse keeper Tom Paterson finished his dinner and cleared the table while his wife hustled all seven of their children off to bed. Tom had been keeping an eye on the storm all day, waiting for it to break. It was a foul night. The lighthouse would be a blessing to any sailor foolish enough, or unlucky enough, to be caught out in this midwinter gale.

Earlier someone had attempted to send a telegraph, but the voice had been unintelligible. The beam from the light cut through the dense fog at regular intervals, illuminating the crashing surf below the lighthouse keeper's home. Tom piled the dishes into the sink.

Outside he heard a scraping sound. He listened. The rain pelted down, the wind howled, the surf roared, but something else had caught his attention. It was coming from the front. He flung open the door.

"Honey!" he hollered to his wife. "We've got two young boys half frozen to death on our front porch. We'll need blankets and hot drinks. These boys look to be a hair's breath away from meeting their Maker!"

James collapsed at Tom's feet. *Saved*! Soon, he and Alexander were sipping hot tea and nibbling on home-made biscuits, wrapped in heavy woollen blankets.

He listened numbly as Alexander told the lighthouse keeper about the *Valencia*. He didn't want to think about Alexander's family or the others on the rocks just three miles away.

Tom Paterson listened silently and when Alexander had finished speaking he got up. "Give me a minute to compose a telegram to the *Victoria Times*."

When he returned, he handed Alexander a piece of paper. "Here," he said, "this is what I sent."

Cape Beale, Vancouver Island, January 23rd (3:35 PM)
To Captain Gaudin, Victoria. Steamer Valencia *ashore in bad place. One hundred on board? Rush assistance. Say Between 50 and 60 drowned.*

T. Paterson, lightkeeper

"Thank you," said Alexander simply.

The lighthouse keeper nodded. "I'm going to escort you to Bamfield." He held up his hand, before anyone could complain. "Don't worry, we will start a full scale search for your family. I know you are at the end of your rope, but someone from the Pacific Cable Station will meet you and take care of you from there."

"No," James protested, jumping up and spilling his tea. "We have to help those left on board. We promised. They are waiting for us out there."

The lighthouse keeper shook his head. "There is nothing you can do now. As we speak, assistance is racing toward the *Valencia*. You've already done all you can."

TEN

Heavy the sorrow that bows the head
When love is alive and hope is dead.

— SIR W.S. GILBERT, *HMS PINAFORE*

"All you can?" I repeated.

The old man sitting across from me wrung his hands. For a long time, he didn't say anything. I found the map above the fireplace and unconsciously traced the zigzagging lines that marked the rugged coastline of Vancouver Island. Cape Beale lay just north of Pachena Point. Below that, by about five miles, lay the Carmanah Point lighthouse and west, across the narrow channel, lay Cape Flattery and the entrance to the Strait of Juan de Fuca.

The sound of the Pacific Ocean, crashing onto the rocky beach and the echo of my great-grandfather's story filled the room.

"It was over for Alexander and myself, but it was

not over for those poor souls waiting for help on the *Valencia*."

He handed me the aged scrapbook. Gingerly, I opened it to the last page. The paper was yellowed, the black ink faded to a mottled grey.

The Vancouver Daily Province
Tuesday, January 23, 1906
Disabled Valencia Went Ashore in Howling Gale
Awful Accident Occurred at Midnight off
Storm-swept Coast of Vancouver Island,
While San Francisco–Vancouver Liner Was On
Her Way North From Golden Gate City.

LIGHTKEEPER CALLS FOR ASSISTANCE
Official Message Says Loss of Life Is Terrible.

"What happened when news of the wreck of the *Valencia* reached Victoria?" I asked, my eyes glued to the morbid headline.

He closed his eyes. "Four ships were immediately despatched. Two tugs — the *Salvor* and the *Czar* — and two steamships — the *Queen City*, out of Victoria and the *City of Topeka*, out of Seattle. None of them carried surf boats."

"Surf boats?" I asked.

"Small boats designed specifically to weather the breakers just off the shoreline, the only kind of boats that could have helped the *Valencia*.

"Did the ships get there on time?"

Great-grandfather's eyes fluttered, but he did not open them. "I often wish Alexander and I had obeyed Captain Johnson's orders and gone straight to Shelter Blight — the cliffs above where the *Valencia* ran aground. The four ships located the *Valencia* the next morning, but...." His voice drifted off and he motioned for me to continue reading. My hand trembled as I turned the page.

The Vancouver Daily Province
Wednesday, January 24, 1906
EXTRA EDITION 1:00 P.M.
ONLY 15 RESCUED FROM VALENCIA
"I Don't Think There Will Be any of the Ship Left."
Is the telegram from the Operator at Bamfield Creek.

BELIEVED THAT 150 PEOPLE ARE DROWNED
Rescue Steamers From Victoria Were Unable to Approach Ill-fated Liner During the Night And She is Believed to Have Gone Down With All on Board. Women and children lost when first boats were launched from the ship's side — electric light plant was put out of action and ship was in darkness.

I stared at the grainy black-and-white article, its strange language and capitalization a token of the past. For a long time I searched for the right words, but my tongue thickened with anguish.

"Only 15 survived?"

"That's what they thought at first. The actual number was 38."

"What about Bosun McCarthy and the men with him?"

"McCarthy managed to stumble to a lineman's cabin at Darling River, just up the telegraph trail. One of the men in his party phoned the lineman in Clooose, a small Native village nearby, who, with the lighthouse keeper from Carmanah, started out toward the *Valencia,* but the going was rough. They arrived at the cliffs above the wreck a full day and a half later.

"What happened?" James asked quietly.

"The *Queen City* did not reach the site of the wreck until nine o'clock that night, 21 hours after the *Valencia* hit the rocks. It was too dark to see anything, so she lay over until the next morning. The weather was thick and the tide was high, the waves cresting at 35 feet or more. All the captain of the *Queen City* could see was the funnel and the remaining mast of the *Valencia* swaying in the wind. The rest of her was gone, buried under the sea."

Great-grandfather paused and swallowed. "There were at least 60 people clinging onto the mast and they cheered when they saw the steamer approaching. Soon after, the *City of Topeka* arrived, with the manager of the Pacific Steamship Company. He ordered the *Queen City* back to Victoria, believing there was nothing she could do. The other three boats stayed behind to look for survivors in the water, but not one of them tried to approach the dying *Valencia.* I don't think, at first, the people on the steamer believed they would just be left there to die, but after a few hours, they realized the horrible truth. Meanwhile, a party of rescuers from Bamfield arrived at the cliffs above the *Valencia*."

"Did they help them?" I asked.

"They couldn't do anything either, except watch the tragedy unfold. It is so rugged out there, they had to crawl on their hands and knees to the edge of the cliff. They had no lifelines to throw to the ship, nor had the *Valencia*. They say there was no panic. The women clinging to the rigging of the nearly submerged ship, simply kept on singing."

Great-grandfather took a raspy breath. I strained to hear the words of the old hymn he crooned.

Nearer, my God, to Thee,
Nearer to Thee!
E'en though it be a cross
That raiseth me.

I could see them out there — their voices weak, their pale bodies fluttering above the raging sea, while all around them the gale howled and beneath them, the poor, battered ship broke up.

"For 48 hours they floated helplessly in the storm. Finally a huge wave crashed into the *Valencia* and swallowed her. Perhaps if Alexander and I had tried earlier, there may have been a chance, but...."

"What a terrible way to die," I shuddered.

Great-grandfather nodded in agreement. "Later on

that afternoon, the *City of Topeka* found a life raft with 20 survivors, barely alive."

"Alexander's family?" I asked, over the lump in my throat.

A barely discernible smile played about his lips. "The lifeboat with Alexander's family in it was swept into Pachena Bay. A Native man assisting in the rescue found them, bruised, nearly frozen, frightened out of their wits, but alive. Alexander was so happy to see them, that he actually cried when he saw the twins and swore he would never think ill of them again!"

"And you, Great-grandfather?"

"I'm here, aren't I?" he replied.

I thumbed slowly through the rest of my great-grandfather's scrapbook, reading report after report of the wreck. Halfway through, he interrupted me. He stood up and shuffled slowly to the window. "She's still out there, you know," he said. "I visit her sometimes, at low tide."

That night, I slept in fits and starts, feeling the shadowy presence of the photo of the *Valencia* glowing in the soft moonlight above my head.

I awoke early, wolfed down a bowl of cereal, pulled on my sandals and headed toward the beach. The going was difficult. In 1907, a year after the wreck of the *Valencia*, a crew of men, at the urging of the government, had begun construction on the Shipwreck Mariner's Trail. My great-grandfather still called it that, but I knew it as the West Coast Trail. It wound its way up the west coast of Vancouver Island, through the dark rainforest, over raging creeks and along the battered beaches, all the way from Port Renfrew to Pachena Bay. I followed my great-grandfather's section of the rough-hewn trail. It was steep and had ladders instead of stairs in some places. I picked my way down slowly. Even though it was low tide and the sea was at her calmest, the salty spray washed over me.

The beach at the bottom was rocky and, as I made my way across the surface, my feet sank into the slick stones.

The Pacific churned and swirled in eddies along the shore. I looked back up the stairs I had just descended. They hugged the cliff face, winding down in tight S turns. I imagined the rescue party peering down from the top. Without the crude stairs, beach access would have been impossible.

My progress over the beach was slow and, as I walked, I thought about the pictures of sunken ships hanging on my great-grandfather's walls. Mostly, I thought about the iron-sided *Valencia* and the small boy staring solemnly from his vantage point in the rigging as the steamer pulled out of San Francisco to begin her journey up the Northwest coast.

The last clipping in my great-grandfather's scrapbook described the final minutes of the doomed steamer:

The Vancouver Daily Province
Thursday, January 24, 1906
BELIEVED THAT 150 PEOPLE
ARE DROWNED

Rescue Steamers From Victoria Were
Unable to Approach ill-fated Liner
During the Night And She is Believed to
Have Gone Down With All on Board.
The Valencia is believed to have gone
to pieces during the night. This information
was received in two despatches at noon.
The first despatch was from Cape Beale, which
says that the rescue Steamers Queen City and
City of Topeka and Salvor arrived last night.
They were unable to get near to the place
where the wreck was supposed to be,
on account of the heavy wind.
A howling gale blew in from the open
ocean during the whole night.

"Valencia," I whispered.

The salty spray washed over me. The cool black stones pulled at my feet.

Fifty feet out, I spotted the wretched bow of the *Valencia* protruding from the violent surf. She looked toward the open ocean. Across the sea spray I thought I saw an ancient wooden lifeboat. It moved at a steady speed, rising on the crests of the waves. Her ghostly crew chanted:

Row, row, row your boat
Gently down the stream.
Merrily, merrily, merrily, merrily,
Life is but a dream.

They rowed the lifeboat over the waves, keeping perfect time with their shattered oars. A skeleton crew, they melted into the mist, replaced by the tragic figure of a young woman clutching a swaying mast, a tiny baby in her arms. She sang a haunting hymn, the dead notes echoing across the water.

I stumbled backward and fell. Something sharp ripped open the soft skin of my hand. I stuck my bleeding palm into my mouth, tasting blood and rust.

There, half-buried in the pebbles, lay a piece of jagged metal. I excavated the weather-beaten square and noticed one corner was red where the tin had pierced my skin.

I turned the curious object over in my hands. Letters were engraved into the thin, metallic surface. Painfully, I scratched years of sand from their raised surface. Etched into the tin were the letters: V A L E N C I A. Underneath the name was painted: NO. 5.

The name board weighed heavily in my cold hands. I climbed the steep stairs, turning my back on the lost souls who wandered the uninhabitable shores of "The Graveyard of the Pacific."

Great-grandfather was making breakfast when I returned. I was out of breath and clutched the tin name board to my chest.

"Here," I said, putting it on the table in front of him.

He picked it up and turned it over slowly. "A year after the wreck, two First Nations boys were out paddling their canoe, near where the *Valencia* sank. They found a large sea cave and inside the cave they discovered one of the *Valencia*'s lifeboats. It had been trapped there by the tide. Number five."

He ran his fingers over the rusted letters and took a deep breath. "Eight skeletons were on board — they died of starvation and exposure, prisoners trapped inside the cliff."

"I know," I whispered.

"I thought you might," he replied. "The *Valencia* is in your blood."

EPILOGUE

On January 22, 1906, the steamship *Valencia* ran aground off Pachena Point, Vancouver Island, in a treacherous area of the west coast called "The Grave-yard of the Pacific." Of the 164 passengers and crew aboard, 38 survived. Only 59 bodies were recovered from the battered shoreline. As Alexander Hamilton, James Moffat and their families exist only in the author's imagination they *do* survive in this story despite the fact that, in reality, no women and children outlived the wreck of the *Valencia*. Early newspaper accounts and the telegraph from the lighthouse cite numbers of victims and survivors on board, at sea and on land, which reflect initial counts, estimates or guesses that were proven inaccurate upon official evaluation and are an example of the typical chaos surrounding early reports from a disaster scene. We have included them here for the purposes of authenticity.

Many vessels have met their end in this rugged

stretch of British Columbia's coastline, but none ended so tragically as the *Valencia*.

Both the Canadian and the American public were outraged by the passive rescue of the boats that witnessed the final moments of the *Valencia*. Also, no rescue equipment was available onshore. A Commission of Inquiry held soon after the sinking resulted in sweeping recommendations. Communication aids and rescue equipment, including surf boats, were installed at close intervals, a lighthouse was built at Pachena Point and the Shipwrecked Mariner's Trail — now known as the world famous West Coast Trail — was constructed.

Three months after the *Valencia* set sail for Vancouver Island, San Francisco was rocked by a horrific earthquake (measuring 8.3 on the Richter scale) and most of the city burned to the ground in the aftermath.

Dead Reckoning is based on factual, historical and eyewitness accounts of the sinking of the *Valencia*. Because of the unpredictable and dangerous shoreline, it took recovery workers months to find all the bodies of the victims. In spite of an intense search, 67 bodies remained unaccounted for and their remains still lie near the *Valencia*. The following summer, in 1907, First Nations paddlers did find a lifeboat from the *Valencia*, with eight skeletons wedged in a cave near where she had run aground and ghost sightings of the steamer, even today, are not uncommon.

Alexander Hamilton and James Moffat exist only in the author's imagination.

Today, people from all over the world come to Vancouver Island to hike the challenging (77 kilometre) West Coast Trail, where, at low tide, the bow of the *Valencia* can still be seen, wedged eternally between two sharp rocks, facing out to the open ocean.

The wreck lies inside Pacific Rim National Park and serves as a natural reef for aquatic sea life that has remained undisturbed for years.

ACKNOWLEDGEMENTS

In researching *Dead Reckoning,* I was able to read many books, articles and news clippings on the wreck of the *Valencia*. I would like to thank Rachel Grant, librarian at the Vancouver Maritime Museum, for her help. In particular, thanks to Leonard McCann, Curator Emeritus at the museum, for his knowledge, patience and generosity in providing me with a quiet place to research and write, as well as a wealth of books.

The following books contain fascinating information, pictures and accounts of the wreck of the *Valencia*: *Pacific Graveyard: A Narrative of Shipwrecks Where the Columbia River Meets the Pacific Ocean* and *Shipwrecks of the Pacific Coast,* both by Jim Gibbs, *Keepers of the Light* by Donald Graham, *The Valencia Tragedy* by Michael Neitzel, *British Columbia Shipwrecks* by T. W. Paterson, *Shipwrecks of British Columbia* by Fred Rogers, *Breakers Ahead! A History of Shipwrecks on the Graveyards of the Pacific* by Bruce R. Scott, *Wreck of the Steamer Valencia: Report to the President by the United States Commission on the Valencia Disaster, Terror on the West Coast* by David Griffiths and *The Valencia Tragedy* by Bill Wolferstan.